Mystery of
The Haunted Pool

By PHYLLIS A. WHITNEY

Cover design by Charles Liese

SCHOLASTIC BOOK SERVICES
New York Toronto London Auckland Sydney Tokyo

Other books by
PHYLLIS A. WHITNEY

The Mystery of the Gulls
Mystery of the Black Diamonds
Mystery on the Isle of Skye
*Mystery of the Green Cat**
Secret of the Samurai Sword

Available from Scholastic Book Services

ISBN: 0-590-08610-3

Copyright © 1960 by Phyllis A. Whitney. This edition is published by Scholastic Book Services, a division of Scholastic Magazines, Inc., by arrangement with The Westminster Press.

22 21 20 19 18 17 16 15 14 13 12 11   0 1 2 3 4 5/8

Printed in the U.S.A.   06

Contents

WITH MANY THANKS to Christine Torgersen, of the Highland Falls Public Library, for introducing me to the people who helped me in gathering material for this book, and also for introducing me to her section of the Hudson River.

My thanks as well to Frank Wallace, of the Fort Montgomery Fire Company, whose enthusiasm for his work, and careful explanation of technical details concerning fires and fire engines, gave authenticity to that phase of the story.

Also a special thank-you to Julia Cobey, of the real "Old Oak," for her generous and friendly assistance.

1

"Something Fishy Going On"

THE AIR-COOLED BUS had followed the west bank of the Hudson River all the way from New York City, and Susan Price had loved every minute of this journey she was taking by herself. Without four brothers along, things seemed very peaceful. The city had been hot and damp and gray, but here the sun was shining, and when the highway curved above the river she could glimpse blue water far below, reflecting the sky of this late afternoon in August.

It wouldn't be long before she reached Highland Crossing, where she was to stay with her aunt, Mrs. Edith Sperry, until the rest of the family joined her in a month or so. That is, they would join her if the house problem was solved.

Dad had grown up in Highland Crossing and he said the Hudson Highlands began where the river narrowed into tight curves and the hills rose steeply on either side. Below the highways she could see the twisting of the river, and now there were hills everywhere—so she must be nearly there.

Thinking of Dad took a little of the joy out of the day. When she had said good-bye to him at the hospital yesterday, he had told her he wanted her to be cheerful no matter how things turned out.

"In a few months you'll be in your teens," he said, "and growing up means learning to take the bad times in your stride, along with the good."

But sometimes it was hard to be cheerful when Dad was in the hospital and when the very things that might help him were still unsettled. It was even a little frightening, because Mom had warned her that the impression she made up here might affect the matter of the house. There were times, Mom reminded her, when Susan had let her imagination run away with her, with astonishing and not always favorable results. She was to see that didn't happen on this visit. As an emissary of the Prices, she must make the best impression possible on Captain Daniel Teague, who, in a sense, held their future in his hands.

Susan pressed her nose against the window as she watched for a sign that would name the town.

It was a freckled nose, and the eyes above it were wide-set and deeply brown. Her short brown hair fluffed out beneath the brim of a straw hat and her white gloves were still almost spotless. Indeed, she could hardly recognize this dressed-up self. It would be good to get outdoors in jeans at Aunt Edith's. When she wore jeans she could almost keep up with Adam, who always set the standard of physical achievement in her life.

Adam! She sighed. He had been disappointed because she had been the one to come on ahead. Adam was her favorite brother, even though he was always the one hardest to please, the one who expected the most of her.

The bus rolled to a smooth stop and the driver called out, "Highland Crossing!" in a voice that startled Susan out of her reverie. Somehow she had missed the sign after all.

She picked up her purse and small suitcase, reached for her book, and arrived at the door in something of a scramble. When she jumped to the ground, the door closed behind her and the bus moved off with a roar of its powerful motor.

Susan stood for a moment in the dirt path along the edge of the paved road, looking up and down uncertainly. Hills rose before her and cut down in a curving line at either side as if they swallowed the highway, and there was no river in sight. Had there been a mistake of some sort? Had she only imagined that the driver had called her stop? There seemed to be no town, but only a gas station a few yards down the road, then a long stretch of lake on this side. Across the highway was a small building with a square white tower topped by some sort of curious red pyramid arrangement. It looked as if it might be a miniature school. But that was all, and there was no Aunt Edith in sight.

Remembering her instructions, Susan began to retrace her steps away from the lake. "If I'm not at the bus stop to meet you," Aunt Edith had written, "just walk back a little way along the road and you'll see the old town hall that is now my shop."

A gigantic oak tree with spreading branches arched above the highway, and as Susan moved toward it the building she was looking for came unmistakably into view. It was big and square and white, with a bracketed roof and a small square tower rising center front. An old-fashioned fan light graced the front door, and on either side of the door were leaded windows that ran almost from baseboard to roof. Just under the eaves was a sign that read "Old Oak Antique Shop" in large, clear letters.

Taking a firmer grip on her suitcase, Susan walked toward the wooden steps that led to the open front door. Just as she reached the steps, a woman came hurriedly out of the building. She was a surprising figure, and Susan couldn't help staring. Her girth was too great for her height so that she had a roly-poly look that did not go very well with the full peasant skirt and bright print blouse she was wearing. Her feet were bare, with painted toenails, and had been thrust into Japanese sandals. On her head was a cone-shaped straw hat that rose to a sharp peak. Beneath it her round, plump face was almost hidden by an enormous pair of jeweled sunglasses cut in a pixie slant. Her costume would have been less astonishing on someone young and slender, but this woman was far from slender, and she was clearly middle-aged.

The sunglasses focused on Susan, and the small, pouting mouth pursed a little more as the woman turned and spoke toward the doorway of the shop.

"The bus has come, Edith!" she called. "Here she is!" Then the sunglasses focused elsewhere and the strange, round figure moved off along the edge of the highway.

Susan forgot her at once, for her aunt had appeared on the steps. She was Dad's older sister and she looked like a smaller, feminine edition of Dad. She was quick-moving, with bright blue eyes and a curly shock of gray hair that framed her face becomingly.

She ran down the steps and engulfed Susan in a quick hug, then held her off to look at her.

"I'm glad you've come, Sue dear. How is your father?"

Susan shook her head. "He's not doing very well. The doctor says it's important for him to get into the country where he won't have to breathe city dust and fumes, and where he can be out in the sun a lot."

"We'll get him here!" Aunt Edith said with warm conviction.

Susan glanced around as she went up the steps toward the door. "I was afraid I was in the wrong place. I was looking for a town, and there doesn't seem to be any."

Aunt Edith laughed as she reached for Susan's suitcase. "I suppose we're hardly more than a village, with the highway running through like Main Street. It's the summer people that keep us going, and their houses and cottages are in the woods up and down the hill. On this side, back of the lake, you'll find quite a settlement, but the trees are so thick you can't see much from the highway. Do come in, dear. I'm sorry I wasn't free to meet you when the bus arrived. I didn't want to rush out and leave Altoona in the shop alone. I hate to say it, but I don't trust her one bit. She snoops. And since I'm not sure what it is she's snooping for, she makes me uncomfortable."

Altoona apparently was the odd-looking woman in the sunglasses, and her name seemed as odd as her appearance.

Aunt Edith drew Susan into the big open hall of the shop. The spacious walls were white, broken by more leaded windows. The ceiling was white too, with long crossbeams. The entire space opened into one great room that ran clear to a wall at the rear, and was filled to the brim with everything imaginable in the way of antiques. As her aunt led the way along a center aisle, Susan had a quick glimpse of graceful old furniture, of cabinets, settees with curved backs, tables loaded with things interesting and beautiful, and plump, glass-shaded lamps. What a fascinating world to explore, when she had time.

But now Aunt Edith was leading her toward a door set in the rear partition, and Susan followed her into the narrow room that apparently served her aunt as living quarters, kitchen, and partly as a storeroom as well, judging by the cartons and boxes piled at one end. Here a straight wooden staircase led upward to a built-in second-story bedroom.

"I hope you won't mind our being crowded for a while," Aunt Edith said. "I moved in here after your uncle died several years ago and I haven't needed much room. But a house will seem wonderful again. As I've written your mother, I'm pretty sure I have the right place for us. Since I'll be moving in with you, I'll be able to help with the rent—and later in buying it, if that's possible. I know the financial situation isn't easy for your parents right now. But if we can get your father well, I'm sure he can find a teaching position within driving distance of Highland Crossing."

She set Susan's suitcase down but went right on talking in her lively, cheerful way.

"I don't mind telling you that it was hard to find a big enough house that was available the year round. I'm having some trouble prying Captain Dan out of it, but I'm nothing if not persistent and I'm counting on you to help me."

This was the thing that worried Susan, but before she could ask more about Captain Daniel Teague, Aunt Edith waved her toward the single flight of stairs.

"Put your things up there, if you like. I've fixed you a cot bed for the time being, and emptied a couple of drawers."

A bell jangled as someone came through the shop door, and as Susan climbed the stairs her aunt went to wait on the customer. In the small room above, Susan pulled off her straw hat and gloves and looked around.

For all that the room was tiny and makeshift, Aunt Edith had furnished it with lovely old things, and her bed had a canopy over its tall four posters. There was a little marble-topped dressing table with an oval mirror above and brass-handled drawers below. A note lay on the left side of the dressing table, and Susan went over to read it.

"This half belongs to Susan Price," the note said. "I hope she won't mind sharing."

Susan smiled and opened a small drawer on her side. The warm summer scent of flowery sachet breathed into the room, and somehow she felt doubly welcomed.

Her aunt's voice reached her from the floor below. "That was Altoona again, but I think I'm rid of her now. When you've washed up, come down and help me fix supper. Then we can talk. The bathroom's at the back. Don't fall into my tub."

Susan opened the white door and stepped into a big, windowed room with a huge tub, large enough to float in, and set up off the floor on huge marble feet. The faucets had once been gilded and were in the shape of a swan's neck. The plug had a chain big enough to hold a police dog.

When Susan was ready she hurried down the steep stairs and found her aunt with a ruffled blue apron around her waist, busily mixing a concoction in a casserole.

"That bathtub belonged to the Vanderbilts once upon a time," she said. "It's one of my treasures. I wouldn't go modern for anything." As she spoke, she put the casserole into the oven. "This will take only a little while to brown. I'm sure you must be starved after that long ride, so we'll have an early supper tonight. There's lettuce in the refrigerator if you'd like to fix a salad."

It was pleasant to feel at home so quickly. When Susan had sliced ripe red tomatoes on their lettuce beds and the table was set with a pink and white cloth that would make any supper look like a party, Aunt Edith brought out the casserole of tuna and macaroni topped with cheese, steaming and savory. There were hot corn muffins too, with country butter to melt in the yellow granules, and cold milk in tall blue hobnail glasses.

Between mouthfuls, Susan asked questions. "Tell me about the Captain's house, Aunt Edith. And about the Captain too."

Aunt Edith buttered a bit of corn muffin as she

talked. "Captain Dan has one of the really wonderful old houses in Highland Crossing. So many of the old places have been torn down. It was built by his grandfather, and he and his grandson, Gene Foster, have been rattling around alone in it this summer. There's been a lot of trouble in the family, and I'm afraid he feels he can't afford to keep the house any longer. So he has practically agreed to rent it to us. And perhaps to let us buy it later on. Though there are some *ifs*."

"If what?" Susan asked.

A twinkle came into Aunt Edith's blue eyes. "*If* he decides that he approves of the Prices as a family. And *if* I can lull him into a state where he won't be so suspicious of me."

"But why would he be suspicious of you?"

"He has a reason. That old house is full of things I'd give anything for. Of course I couldn't really afford to buy them all, but I could sell some of them for him on commission and make a profit for both of us, if only he'd let me. However, it's almost impossible to coax anything out of him, even for a good price. He has his guard up against me."

"What's his grandson like?" Susan asked.

"Gene?" Aunt Edith drew her brows into a thoughtful frown. "That's a long story. And rather a sad one. Gene has been in and out of hospitals ever since an accident two years ago. He's a little older than you, I think—about thirteen. Gene is one of the stumbling blocks in the whole plan. He's bitterly set against moving out of the house and his grandfather's been reluctant to hurt him with the move. If you can make friends with Gene, it might help. But he's a difficult boy to be friendly with."

She sighed and changed the subject to something more cheerful.

"Your mother writes me that you're quite a reader, so I suppose you'll want to take out a card in our library soon. We have a new branch here in Highland Crossing that we're very proud of."

Susan brightened. "Dad said he didn't think there was a library here, and I was wondering what I'd do without one."

"It's very close—just across the highway, hardly a block away. It's a new venture this year, run on a volunteer basis, with the librarian from the next town upriver supervising the work. It's open from two to five every afternoon, and some of the women in town take turns at the desk to help out, since we have no money yet for a real librarian. The Girl Scout troop goes in once a week and keeps everything clean. It's small, but there's a good book collection loaned to us by the big library."

This sounded like fun, and Susan was about to ask more questions when Aunt Edith looked up suddenly, listening. "Is that someone in the shop? Sometimes people don't notice the bell pull and just walk in. Sue dear, will you run and look while I dish up the dessert?"

Susan left the table and walked into the big room that had once been a town hall. With a little start, she saw that something had happened to the lighting of the room since she had first entered it an hour or so earlier. Outside the high windows, the shadows of early evening were long, and trees shaded the building, so that it had grown dusky inside. Probably the hills above the highway helped to cut off the light too, as the sun went down in the west. In the gloom the unfamiliar room seemed suddenly filled with patches of impenetrable darkness.

Clear across the crowded expanse, the door stood innocently open, and there was no one in sight. Just the same, with all these old pieces of furniture and statuary and oddities, an army might hide around any corner and be quite invisible. With the heightened acuteness of her senses, Susan had the curious feeling that something *was* hiding in the shadows. Something that lived and breathed and moved.

Across the room a book fell to the floor with a clap, and Susan gasped and thrust a hand over her mouth. At the same moment a slithery black shadow streaked up the aisle past her, and this time she squealed out loud.

Aunt Edith came quickly to the rear door and touched a switch. At once the shadows vanished. There was no hidden enemy and Susan's teeth were clearly chattering for nothing.

"A—a book fell off that table by itself," she quavered. "And one of the shadows ran down the aisle."

Aunt Edith laughed and reached to scoop something up from behind a chair. "Here's your shadow," she said, and held up a limp black cat. "It's only

Boneless. He was probably the guilty party who knocked the book down. Don't roll those yellow eyes at me, Bony, my pet. I'll let you go when you've said hello to Susan."

The cat made no effort to resist when Aunt Edith held him out and Susan took him into her hands, aware at once of where he got his name. Boneless flowed into her grasp, hanging as limp as his name. Only his warmth and a deep inner purring revealed that he was alive and not displeased with this attention.

Aunt Edith went to pick up the fallen book and set it back on the stack beside a barrel she had apparently started to unpack.

"Altoona has an eye on these books," Aunt Edith said. "Somehow the word got round that I'd coaxed Captain Dan into letting me take this barrel of old books out of his attic to sell in my shop, and she was down here like a flash wanting to buy the whole thing from me, sight unseen. And for a ridiculously high sum. That made me suspicious. If I'm to make any money for the Captain, and for me as well, I want to know what I'm selling. She was quite annoyed with me because I wouldn't let her go through the barrel first herself. Come on back to your dessert before it melts, and I'll tell you about Altoona."

Aunt Edith didn't bother to close the outer door as she led the way back to the living quarters. Susan put Boneless down and he melted away at once, invisible and as soundless as the shadow she had taken him for.

The story of Miss Altoona Heath was an odd one. Susan ate spoonfuls of vanilla ice cream topped with raspberry sauce, and listened to her aunt's account.

Altoona had been given her odd name because her grandfather had come from a city of that name in Pennsylvania. Aunt Edith had gone to school with her long ago, when that small building with the tower that Susan must have noticed on the highway had been a schoolhouse, instead of the firehouse that it was now. Aunt Edith had always been a little sorry for the plump, rather timid girl with the domineering father and no mother. True, Altoona had an older sister who had more or less brought her up, but the sister was just like the father and there was no affection in either of them.

The family had always been well off, and they lived in a house that was still considered a mansion. But everybody had said poor Altoona would never get a penny and never be allowed to call her soul her own. Then a few years ago there had been a boating accident on the river. Both old Mr. Heath and his elder daughter had drowned, and Altoona had come into everything.

"It was almost pitiful to see her at first," Aunt Edith said. "Those two had never been kind to her, and she hardly knew how to breathe for herself. The only thing in the world she knew anything about was old furniture—because her house was full of it, and she had sometimes borrowed books from me to read about old things. So when it really came home to her that she was rich and could do exactly as she liked she began to collect antiques."

"That must have been good for your business," Susan said.

Aunt Edith smiled wryly. "Not exactly. Altoona has more time on her hands than I have and she began to—well, sort of compete with me. Several times now she's beaten me to some bargain I was after, and I do believe that's the most fun she's ever had in her life. I suppose I shouldn't begrudge it, but she gets under my skin a little sometimes. She's changed so much that she makes me uneasy. I don't really know her any more."

"Does she always dress like that?" Susan asked.

"A bit extreme, isn't she?" Aunt Edith said. "Her father would have had a fit over those clothes and painted toenails. But Altoona is in revolt for the first time in her life, and I expect it has gone to her not very steady head. I only wish I knew why she's so interested in those old books of the Captain's. There's something fishy going on that I don't understand. And somehow I don't like it."

2

The Boy in the Woods

THAT EVENING passed pleasantly in Aunt Edith's cozy living quarters. When the night grew really dark, she took Susan into the shop to show her the old-fashioned carriage lamps she had placed in each of the tall front windows. The "flames" that lighted them were electric bulbs, but they glowed with a warm golden radiance—a welcoming light to the passerby.

"It's nice here," Susan said. "There's only one thing that disappoints me about Highland Crossing so far. I haven't seen the Hudson since I arrived."

"The river's there," Aunt Edith said, moving about the shop to check the locks on each window before closing up for the night. "But it's some distance below us. There are woods and a steep, rocky cliff between us and the water. Not much room for houses there. Though the Teague place has a wonderful view all up and down the river. Tomorrow, if you like, you can do a bit of exploring, and perhaps pay the Captain a visit. I think you'll make a good impression on him."

Later on, while Susan was taking a bath in the magnificent Vanderbilt tub, she thought about tomorrow's plans. And she thought about them again when she snuggled under a light blanket in the cot beside Aunt Edith's big bed. Tomorrow might be rather exciting, and perhaps a little frightening because of Captain Dan and his grandson. Especially the latter, who was set against letting the Prices have his house.

She began to think about home, too, and about her brothers. Duncan was the oldest. He was sixteen and away working on a New England farm this summer. Dunc spent so much time with his head in a science book, or at lab experiments, that Dad had said he needed to get out and use his muscles for a couple of months. Dunc hadn't minded, but he had taken the science books along. Stan and Richie were the youngest, nine and eight respectively, though the way they bossed their one sister, you'd have thought them her seniors. Stan was mostly noisy and rambunctious these days, and his interests changed from one minute to the next. Richie was a darling and still didn't mind being cuddled and read to. Both boys were a handful at home this summer, since there was no money for camps. That was another reason for getting out of New York. Adam had stayed home to help with the boys.

Adam—there he was again in her thoughts, and she could only wish that he hadn't been so disappointed about not coming up here ahead of the family. Adam was fourteen, with thick, reddish hair and eyes that had a flash to them. He was the best-looking one in the family, and he was the strongest too. No one ever had to worry about his muscles. He was wonderful at games and sports and readily popular with other boys. But he not only asked the best possible performance of himself—he also expected it of his friends as well. And of his sister! She would be glad to be alone up here for a little while, even though she would miss Adam.

She wondered about Gene Foster, Captain Dan's grandson, and hoped he would be someone Adam would like. Adam would want friends around right away when he arrived, and it would help if Susan knew some boys to introduce him to. What had Aunt Edith meant about his being hurt a couple of years ago? She had intended to ask about that and had forgotten. Would Gene like Adam?

With all these thoughts, it was a long while before Susan fell asleep.

When she awoke, the sun was coming up in a bright, clear sky. Aunt Edith's alarm went off promptly at six thirty. Susan stayed in bed until her aunt was out of the bathroom, and then hastened to get up herself. She dressed in a blue shirt and a pair of jeans so she could be comfortable outdoors.

"Early morning is the best time for me to accomplish odd jobs," Aunt Edith said. "So I like to rise early and have at a few things."

She "had at" them with a will, whipping up pancakes for breakfast, opening all the windows so the early morning breeze could blow through the shop before the day turned warm, setting down food for Boneless, and stirring around like a small, lively tornado. Susan's father had once said that his sister Edith was a pint-size package of dynamite, and Susan remembered that now.

She offered to help her aunt with the dusting when the breakfast dishes were done, but was waved away.

"I have a woman who comes in part time to help me," Aunt Edith said. "I'll give you a few chores later on, if you like, and I'll appreciate your help. But this is your morning to explore. Just watch out for the cars on the highway—it's difficult to cross. That's how Gene Foster got hurt a couple of years ago. Perhaps this first morning you'd better go downhill toward the river and the Teague house. I want you to visit Captain Dan. There's a dirt road that runs right past the shop downhill."

"How do I find the house?" Susan asked, feeling a little uneasy. She wasn't sure her courage was up to meeting the formidable Captain right away.

"It's easy to find," Aunt Edith said. "Downhill a little way you'll come to a Y in the road. The right-hand branch drops down a steep hill to the boat club on the river. The left-hand fork is a more level road that will lead you right past Captain Dan's house. It's the only house you'll see in that section, and you'll know it by all the pointed turrets and odd levels of roof. Run along now, and I'll expect you home for lunch around twelve."

"Where does Miss Heath live?" Susan asked.

"You might as well call her Miss Altoona, the way the rest of the town does," Aunt Edith said. " 'Miss Heath' still means her sister to most of us. The Heath place is near the other end of the lake. You can see it from the highway."

Susan still hesitated. "But what am I supposed to say to the Captain?"

"He'll take care of that," her aunt told her. "Just go in and announce yourself. He won't bite."

Not altogether reassured, Susan went outside and turned toward the dirt road that led downhill. At once she encountered a surprise. Last night she had not gone around to this side of the house, so she had not discovered that a wide lawn ran along one side of the shop. Between the edge of the grass and the road was an ingenious "fence" made entirely of hitching posts in the shape of white horses' heads, the rings in their mouths connected by strands of painted white chain. Inside this enclosure was an amazing collection of statuary, urns, and garden furniture, all grouped around a small octagonal summerhouse. There were busts of whiskered gentlemen whom Susan did not recognize. There were several snarling lions, nearly life-sized, and a handsome, silver-winged griffin right out of *Alice's Adventures in Wonderland*. But the figure she liked best was a lovely marble girl on a pedestal. The girl held a marble lyre in her hands, and the veined marble of her robe fell in soft folds to her small alabaster feet. Susan reached out to touch the smooth, cool marble of her gown as she went by.

All these things must be for sale in her aunt's shop, and they probably helped to advertise it, collected here on the lawn. But now she must get on with her trip of exploration.

She rounded a big hydrangea bush, thick with lavender blooms, and followed the edge of the road where Queen Anne's lace grew higher than her waist. Strange to think of these white flowers as only weeds, when they were pretty enough to put into a vase.

The earth was dry and powdery, rising in little puffs as she walked along. Now she could see widely spaced houses in the back-of-the-lake area. At the fork she stood for a moment, looking down toward the boathouse. Then she chose the left-hand path that would lead her to Captain Dan's. She began to walk more and more slowly, however. What if the Captain had no wish to see her? Or what if he disapproved of girls who wore jeans? Perhaps she should have dressed up for this visit.

Having thus increased her uncertainty about meeting the Captain, she was ready enough to be beguiled into following a new path that opened at one side of the road. It was a narrow trail, brown with pine needles and crumbling leaves, and it wound down through thick woods in the direction of the river. Susan found herself unable to resist it.

Perhaps she would follow it for just a little way to find out where it went. She could always come back to Captain Dan's later on.

Not many people used this path, for in places

where the earth was bare of leaves, there was a green-velvet covering of moss. Almost at once the woods closed around her and the air was still except for the rustle of a breeze in the treetops far above. She had a feeling that all her city-deadened senses were opening to this lovely summer morning in the woods. She reached out to touch the rough bark of a tree and then upward to let a green tuft of pine prickle the tips of her fingers. And she listened with delight to sounds she was just learning to distinguish. When she was quiet she could hear the faint plunk of pine needles dropping. Now and then birds chattered, and there was a faint sound of humming insects all about.

Then a new sound came to her through the trees —an odd intrusion of sound that seemed familiar, yet did not belong to this setting. It was an irregular sound—a loud plop, followed by a dull, repeated thudding, as if something bounced across dry leaves. This was followed by the noise of something moving around in the woods below.

What in the world was going on? She followed the path around its next steep curve and came upon an unexpected and surprising sight.

The woods opened onto a space of level ground backed by a huge outcropping of rock in the direction of the river. A lone pine tree grew in the embrasure of rock, and high on its trunk a barrel hoop had been nailed. Below the hoop stood a boy with a basketball in his hands. No wonder the sound had seemed familiar. The boy in blue jeans stood with his back to Susan and, as she watched, he hurled the ball toward the improvised basket. The shot was high and it bounced off the natural rock wall above and rolled away to the edge of the woods. The boy made an angry sound as the ball missed. He did not go leaping after it as Adam would have done, but instead moved painfully, swinging his left leg stiffly as he covered the ground. Susan saw the flash of the brace on his foot and knew that it must encase his leg up under the jeans.

Awkwardly he bent to pick up the ball. Then clearly still determined, he hobbled to the barrel hoop and raised his hands for another throw. Susan held her breath, willing the ball to go through the hoop. But this time it merely bounced off the rim and fell back toward the boy. He made a vain attempt to catch it, lost his balance, and fell full length upon the ground with a dismaying thud. The ball rolled away in Susan's direction, and she picked it up uncertainly.

She expected the boy to roll over and struggle back on his feet. But instead he lay where he was, his fists clenched upon the ground. His head rested in the curve of one arm, and she saw to her distress that his shoulders were shaking as if silent sobs of frustration racked him. Almost as keenly as though it had happened to her, Susan knew what he was feeling. He must have been trying for some time to overcome the handicap of his brace-stiffened leg and make the basket. In the end the brace had defeated him, thrown him to the ground, and he had given in to despair. Yet this boy had a good deal of courage. She had seen the evidence.

She must get away quietly and quickly, Susan thought, before he discovered that someone had witnessed his humiliation. She tried to put the ball soundlessly on the ground, but leaves crunched, and the boy raised his head sharply and looked around at her. It was a moment for doing something quickly—almost anything. She went toward him and held out the ball, as if there was nothing wrong.

"You almost made it the last time," she said. "Go ahead and try again. If you'll let me play too, I'll help you chase it when the ball rolls off."

For just a moment she was afraid he would shout at her angrily to go away and leave him alone. He was looking at her with brooding gray eyes, clouded now by despairing tears, and his mouth was twisted in a grimace of pain. Perhaps he had hurt his bad leg further in his fall. But there was also a look of stubbornness about his chin. Slowly, painfully, he struggled to his feet and Susan, watching, suppressed the desire to run and help him. This was a show of courage greater than she had ever seen healthy Adam display, and she knew he must succeed alone. Quite simply and suddenly she wanted very much to have this boy for her friend.

When he stood soundly on his feet again, she brought the ball to him, and he took it without a word and limped back to his place below the basket. While she watched, he aimed carefully, with a great display of coolness, though he must have been quivering with tension inside. His hands and arms obeyed him as his legs would not. The ball made a clean arc through the air and dropped neatly through the basket.

"That was a perfect shot!" Susan cried in delight. "I wish I could do that. Will you teach me how?" She sprang after the ball, before it could bounce off into the woods, and brought it back to him.

Now that he was on his feet, she saw that he was fairly tall and a bit too thin. His face had the peaked look of someone who had been ill. All sign of tears had vanished, brushed hastily away, and he was looking at her with a suspicious scowl, as though he felt she might be making fun of him.

She tried again. "My brother Adam's a whiz at basketball, but he gets impatient with me when I try for baskets. He thinks I'm a butterfingers. I'd like to show him—if you'd help me."

What followed was surely the strangest period of basketball practice that had ever been conducted. The boy with the leg brace was really quite good when he wasn't wound up with intensity. Now that Susan was there to retrieve the ball when he missed, he began to relax, and his aim was sound a remarkable percentage of the time. He even unwound enough to show her the best way to hold the ball, and how to flex her wrists for the throw. When she finally managed to drop a shot through the hoop, he actually smiled at her, and his thin face lighted into surprising warmth.

When they had played until both were winded

and Susan's brown fluff of hair curled in damp tendrils over her forehead, they sat down almost companionably on a ledge of rock and rested. The boy volunteered no conversation, but Susan was not one to stay silent for long.

"Do you live around here?" she asked.

He nodded. "I live in a house up on the rim of the cliff with my grandfather. You can't see it from here because the woods are in between. It's been our family house for generations, but we may have to move out pretty soon. A New York City family is coming to live in our place. Unless I can figure out some way to stop them."

Susan swallowed the words she had been about to speak. This boy was Captain Dan's grandson, and he looked so thoroughly angry about the family who might move into his house that she did not dare to tell him her own identity.

"Why is your grandfather going to let city people move into his house if you want to live in it yourselves?" she asked, trying to sound casual.

The frown deepened on Gene's forehead. "Because of me. Because I was stupid and careless and got myself hit by an automobile up on the highway. It needn't have happened—it was my own fault. So most of the money Grandfather saved has gone for hospital and doctor bills. My mother had to go to work in New York and she's in debt because of me."

He sounded so bitter that Susan was a little frightened. It seemed unlikely that this boy would

ever like any of the Prices—and that included her.
He was disturbing to listen to.

"What about your father?" she asked. "Can't he
help?"

Gene's answer was short. "My father is dead."

"I—I'm sorry," she said, wishing she had not
asked the question.

He would not accept her sympathy. "It's nothing
to you," he told her sharply.

Susan spoke up with a little more spirit. "My
father's in the hospital now. And I've thought of
how awful it would be if—if anything—" She
couldn't go on, but she did have a means of
sympathizing with what Gene must have been
through. "Anyway," she said, "an accident could
happen to anyone. Maybe you shouldn't blame
yourself so much."

He shook his head. "I didn't look where I was
going, and the driver didn't have a chance to miss
me. So here I am—and my mother and my grandfather have to go without things to make up
for one little careless moment. I don't know how
I can stand it if Grandfather has to give up his
home. You don't know how much he loves that
house."

So Gene wasn't thinking just of his own unhappiness and lack of well-being. His grief over
what might happen to his grandfather was all the
more painful to see. Nevertheless, there was something wrong about his blaming himself so furiously.

She stood up, studying the great outcropping of
rock that towered over them. Its sides were slanting

and its ledges and irregularities offered numerous toe holds. It would be fun to climb that rock. She was sure Adam would have climbed it before this. There would probably be a wonderful view of the river from the top.

Before the boy knew what she was about to do, she had taken a running leap at the rock and managed to scamble up it a few feet. There she clung, holding onto a ledge over her head, searching for the next good place to put a foot. But before she could find it, Gene Foster shouted at her.

"Come down!" he ordered. "Get off that rock!"

She thought he was worried about her safety. "I'm a good climber," she called to him. "I won't fall. I'd like to go to the top and have a look at the river."

His voice quivered with strain when he spoke. "I don't care if you break your neck, but you stay off that rock. It's private property. I don't let anybody climb up there."

Susan looked down at him in astonishment. He sounded so bad-tempered and unreasonable that she had a good mind to show him she would do as she pleased. There was no reason for him to talk to her like that. She turned her back on him and climbed to the next ledge, paying no attention to his words. Beneath her she heard the clank of his brace as he stumped with reckless hurry over to the base of the rock.

"If you go one step higher, I'll come after you and haul you down!" he called.

He actually looked as though he would try to

make good his threat. She hesitated, though not because she was afraid of him. With two good legs she could escape him easily. In fact, she doubted that he could really climb more than a foot or two up the face of the rock. But that was the very thing that stopped her. If he tried and failed, then he might fall and hurt himself again. And he would be doubly defeated. It was a risk she had no wish to take even though he was behaving badly.

"All right," she said, "I'll come down."

And down she came, jumping somewhat crossly to the ground. She had humored him, but now she felt ruffled herself and unwilling to spend any more time in his company. One thing was certain. Adam would never want Gene Foster for a friend. And it seemed unlikely that Gene would ever accept the Piicco. If the problem of getting Dad to Highland Crossing was to be solved, everything now depended on Gene's grandfather.

She walked across the clearing without a word and found her way back to the path that opened uphill. Before she had taken six steps, she was dying to look behind and see what Gene thought of her haughty retreat. It would serve him right if he was sorry to see her go. But there was complete silence behind her, and she knew it would spoil the dignified effect of her departure if she looked around.

3

The Upside-down Tree

THE PATH climbed more steeply than she remembered, and before she had gone very far she realized that she had mistaken another opening in the woods for the one through which she had descended. This path climbed upward between trees that grew precipitously out of the rocky cliff. The boy did not call to her to come down this time, and since the path turned in the right direction, she continued to follow it. Not being used to hills, she was puffing a little when she came out into a pleasant, woodsy glen on level ground above.

A short distance to her left rose a faded green house with a strange assortment of cupolas and

30

towers that could only be the house of Captain Daniel Teague. Springy grass covered the small clearing, and on her right a quiet pool stretched away as if to hide itself where the woods began.

Once more she postponed facing the Captain. First she must look at this enchanting woodland pool. Because of the shadowing trees that overhung it, the water looked almost black toward the far side. Around the nearest edge a thin scum covered the water, turning it emerald green. Yet it was not a stagnant pool, for Susan could see the place where a little brook opened into it, running only a trickle of water now, though perhaps in spring it would be a rushing stream.

Not far from where she stood a fallen log pointed a brown finger out into the pool, and Susan stepped onto it. It seemed steady enough, and she edged out a little upon its length. Away from the bank there was no scum, and she could see the stones on the bottom of the pool in this fairly shallow place. Her own face gazed back at her, with ripples stirring her hair, as if a wind lifted it. Tiny water spiders skittered about on the surface, and she watched them for a while in fascination. She was aware of how quiet the woods were, and of how lonely it seemed here, in spite of the house that raised its towers near at hand. She had the strange feeling that this was a place of secrets. The sense of mystery and loneliness began to make her uncomfortable. Perhaps it would be just as well if she went to make the acquaintance of Captain Daniel Teague before his disagreeable grandson returned.

As she walked toward the rear of the house, meaning to circle it before she went up the front walk, she was stopped once more by the sight of a most curious tree. It seemed to be growing upside down. From its high, uppermost tip, all its branches grew downward, instead of up. They trailed thick and blue-dark clear to the ground, closing around the trunk like the sloping sides of a tent. She had never seen such a tree, and it amazed and interested her. Behind those drooping branches there must be a hidden place close to the trunk —a secret, shaded place, shielded completely from view.

As she watched, she caught an unexpected movement among the branches. Something was fumbling behind them. Before her eyes, a hand reached out and parted the leaves. Into this opening was thrust the peak of a straw beach hat. The hat came through completely, then tilted upward a little to reveal a pair of sunglasses beneath the brim. While Susan stood frozen in astonishment, the glasses seemed to study the Teague house in a calculating manner that did not fit their gay pixie slant. Then the hat withdrew into its shelter, the plump hand allowed the branches to fall back in place, and the tree stood dark and silent as though nothing had ever disturbed it.

Now why was the odd Miss Altoona Heath spying on the Captain's house?

Not at all sure what she ought to do, but reluctant to have Miss Altoona see her, Susan walked quickly around to the front of the house, avoiding the upside-down tree. Once out of sight, she stood for a few moments on the walk, looking up at the house where she and her family might eventually live. Her heart began to beat more quickly in pleasant anticipation, and once more she forgot Miss Altoona.

She loved the house on sight—loved every balcony and pointed tower and gingerbread curlicue. She loved the wide, old-fashioned veranda that ran across the front and clear around one side, loved the feeling of something old and dignified and rich in history.

The house was set upon a high foundation wall above ground, and she went up the steep flight of front steps and stood on the veranda. The front door with its oval glass panel stood open, and she could look inside through the screen door. The builder had apparently dispensed with an entry hall. Or perhaps the entire living room had been intended as the sort of baronial hall Susan had read about in books. Along the far side a shadowy staircase ran upward, to divide at a landing and rise left and right to a second-floor balcony that seemed to overlook part of the living room.

But she could not stand here staring into the house without making her presence known. She could not find a bell, but discovered an ancient knocker on the outside of the door. The decorative iron knob made a startling clamor as she brought it down against its plate. Listening to the echoes die away, she began to worry about Captain Dan. She wished she had asked her aunt more about him. If he was as black-tempered and difficult as his grandson, she wasn't sure she wanted to face him.

Having made all that noise, however, there was nothing to do but wait. At length she heard the sound of someone moving inside, and a woman's voice called to her a bit testily.

"Well, don't stand there, child! The door's open—come on in and save my legs the trip downstairs."

Thus instructed, Susan opened the door and stepped into the wide, high-ceilinged living room. She had a quick glimpse of a darkly polished floor with small rugs scattered here and there, of old-fashioned furniture, and a huge open fireplace at one end. The room was paneled in reddish mahogany, and a long mirror was set into the wall on either side of the marble mantel. On other walls were seascapes and Hudson River scenes. But she had no time to study them, for through the gloom of the big room she saw the woman who had spoken watching her from the balcony opposite the door.

Her head was done up in a blue kerchief with the ends knotted in front. She wore a bibbed blue apron about her ample waist, and one hand held a dustcloth, the other a mop.

"Is—is Captain Teague at home?" Susan asked, wishing more than ever that she had not ventured this visit without her aunt. "I'm Susan Price. My aunt—"

"Oh, so you're Tom Price's daughter? I knew your pa when he was knee-high to a grasshopper. I'm Mrs. Bancroft, the Captain's housekeeper. Yes —he's home. Just follow the veranda around to the back and you'll see the steps down cellar. You'll find him in his workshop. No need to announce yourself—just run along."

Susan said thank you to Mrs. Bancroft and retreated through the screen door. The veranda was comfortably wide, with several chairs facing the rail. At the rear it continued its circling of the house, though it narrowed at the back. Following it around, Susan forgot to look for the cellar steps, for at last she had a full view of the Hudson River.

The cliff fell away steeply below the house, and the tops of trees made a thick green sea plunging down the hill. But except for the single tree that grew upside down, the foliage was lower than the house back here, and beyond it the Hudson River curled past, flowing calmly, quietly on its old, old way from Albany to the sea. Hills rose above the far bank and she could see the long span of what must be the Bear Mountain Bridge on her right. A string of lighters was drifting lazily downriver, hardly seeming to move, though the chugging of their tug came to her distantly across the water.

She had known the river all her life, living in New York, but somehow she had always taken it for granted. Now it seemed to have a different character—to be a river she had never seen before. She thought of the stories she had read that had made Hudson history. Tales by Washington Irving of Rip Van Winkle and Ichabod Crane. Stories of the general, Mad Anthony Wayne, of the haunted Dunderberg, even of Henry Hudson, the mighty sailor who had given his life as well as his name to the great river. Not until the prickles of excitement had subsided a little did Susan remember the cellar stairs.

She found them easily and went hesitantly down into a big furnace room, off which other rooms opened. Since there were windows above ground all the way around, the basement seemed lighter than the gloomy living room upstairs. Through a nearby open door came the sound of someone moving about. Susan stepped to the doorway and looked in.

This was the neatest, most shipshape workshop she had ever seen. Tools hung in precise order on a big wooden panel. Machinery of one sort or another was tidily arranged, the work bench unlittered except for materials in use. Before the bench, half turned away from her, stood a man in blue slacks and a light-blue shirt. He was of medium height, but he stood tall, and his shoulders were erect. A fringe of gray hair grew about his balding head, making little feathery tufts on either side just above his ears. The eyes he turned upon her were gray and steady.

"Are—are you Captain Teague?" Susan faltered.

"I am," he admitted gravely, as though her sudden appearance did not surprise him in the least. "How do you like my workshop?"

"It looks as though you have everything," she said, and thought how Adam would love such a room.

He nodded. "Just about. I used to keep things around the house in order myself, but I find it's all getting a bit too much for me lately."

Did that mean he might want to be out of the house? she wondered hopefully. At least he was not as frightening as she had expected, nor as unfriendly as his grandson.

He gestured toward a large piece of white cardboard on which he had been painting colored letters. "Tell me what you think of it. Will it get attention, do you suppose?"

Relieved to be asked no question more personal, Susan stared at the brightly lettered sign that read FYRE FYTERS FROLIC. Feeling that such a sign would certainly attract attention, she nodded her approval.

"That's fine," Captain Dan said. "I was hoping somebody would show up to give me an opinion. Now when I get the date lettered in, it will be all set to go. A good thing it is you'll be here for the fair, Susan. I've a notion you'll enjoy it."

Susan looked at him in wonder. "How did you know who I am?"

He picked up his paintbrush and went back to work. "I've been expecting you. Your Aunt Edith phoned a while ago and said you might be down this way. And I am glad to see one of the Prices for myself." The keen gray eyes studied her as if there was not very much that they missed. "I suppose you're wondering why I'm painting a sign like this," he went on.

She hadn't had much time to wonder, but since he seemed to be inviting her interest, she nodded again.

"I'll tell you," he said, needing little encouragement. "I'm chief of the Volunteer Fire Company of Highland Crossing. Have been for the last ten years, in fact."

"Is that why people call you 'Captain'?" Susan asked.

"Not exactly. My title in the fire company is 'Chief.' I used to be captain of a boat that sailed the Hudson River between New York and Albany. Captains run in our family. My great-grandfather, old Captain Rufus Teague, was the first one. He sailed a clipper ship to China in the old days. When clippers went out and steam took over, we had Teagues sailing freighters and liners on the Atlantic and the Pacific. Of course I was something of a disappointment to my father when I didn't hanker after the ocean."

He bent to give close attention to the letter he was forming, then went on.

"I was born in this house, right in sight of the Hudson, and I guess the river's in my blood. Oceans don't have anything to say to me. I like to see a shore line sliding by. But you needn't think it's an easy trick taking a ship up the Hudson. A river sailor doesn't have a whole ocean to maneuver in, or the depth of many fathoms under him."

Captain Dan pulled up a high wooden stool and gestured Susan toward it. When she had climbed up on the perch and hooked her heels over a rung, she asked another question.

"Was Gene's father a captain too?"

"Well, now—that was a queer sort of business when you come to think of it. I had to break the line of captains by having a daughter instead of a son. But when my girl grew up, what did she do but marry Captain Foster, who flew a plane in the last war, and was an airline pilot later on. So we kept on with captains in the family until he was killed in a crash a few years back."

"I met your grandson a little while ago down in the woods," Susan told him.

"Did you, now? And what did you think of him?"

That was hard to say. Especially to his grandfather.

"He was practicing with a basketball," she explained. "And he let me play for a while. Then when I wanted to climb a big rock to see if I could glimpse the river, he got angry and told me to get down. So I left him and came up here."

The Captain concentrated intently on the final *t* in the word "August." Susan wondered if her indignation had sounded in her voice, and if perhaps he was annoyed with her for walking off and leaving his grandson.

"I—I tried to be friends with him," she added apologetically.

"Don't try too hard if he isn't nice to you," he told her. "The trouble with Gene is that he's been spoiled a bit in hospitals and then at home with his mother. He has a notion everybody's got to jump in circles to please him because he's got a bad leg. It's just as well his mother is working and couldn't be with him this summer. When I took over, he couldn't move anyplace without crutches. But I've been pushing him to try a little harder every day. I put up that hoop for him, and I'm glad to hear he's working with the basketball."

"But what good will it do? I mean, can he ever really play basketball?"

"The doctors say not," Captain Dan told her frankly. "But I claim this is something a fellow has to work out for himself. That's one reason in favor of having you Prices move up here. I remember your dad as a boy, and I think his four sons might be good for Gene to have around."

"But what will you do when we move in? I mean, will you stay here too?"

"No—we've got a cabin down in the woods where you saw Gene playing. We'd have to rough it a bit and leave Mrs. Bancroft to take care of the house for your mother. She's had a houseful of boys herself—grown up now—and she's used to kids. But I expect we'd be coming back and forth, and Gene would be thrown in with your brothers whether he liked it or not."

Susan thought about this in silence, wondering how much good the Price boys would do Gene. Duncan wouldn't pay much attention to him unless he was interested in science. Stan was at the rough-house stage, and while Richie was sweet to everybody, he would be a bit young as a friend for Gene. And Adam—? She squirmed uneasily, thinking how little Adam was likely to be interested in anyone who couldn't keep up with him in climbing and in sports. Especially a boy who didn't want to be friends in the first place. But she did not want to say any of this to the Captain. It would be better, perhaps, to change the subject to something safer.

"Aunt Edith is looking forward to moving up

here," she said. "She's crazy about old houses. In fact, about all sorts of old things. She says your place is full of treasures."

The Captain threw her a quick look, and she saw that his eyes could turn to a chilly gray all in a moment, and that his chin, too, might have a stubborn set to it. He had finished his sign and he wiped off the paintbrush carefully before he spoke.

"You might as well know that I haven't made up my mind yet about letting this house out of my hands. And I don't mind telling you that your Aunt Edith scares me a little. I can holler at a man if I have to. With a man I can lay down the law if that's what's called for. But laying down the law with your aunt is like telling the wind not to blow. Maybe I just want to hang onto all the stuff in this house. Now take that old barrel of books in the attic, for instance. I can't think of one good reason why I let her take those off to sell. But she came down here yesterday like a whirlwind, and when I picked myself up and collected my wits, she'd talked me out of that batch of books. I suspect a man isn't safe around your Aunt Edith."

He sounded as though he was only half joking, and his eyes still looked cool, but before Susan could think of anything to say, an outraged voice spoke from the doorway of the workshop.

"You *didn't* let Mrs. Sperry have that book barrel from the attic!" the voice said accusingly.

Susan whirled about on her stool. Gene Foster stood in the doorway, balancing awkwardly on his stiff, brace-encased leg. A scowl puckered his forehead and his eyes were stormy dark.

Captain Dan looked at him calmly. "Well now, your honor, it's guilty I seem to be. Mrs. Sperry had a notion that old books in an attic would do nobody any good. She offered to look through them and see if there was anything there worth selling. And I didn't seem to be able to argue with her at the time. All my reasons *why not* seemed to make no sense while she was here dinging away at me."

"You had no right—" Gene began, but his grandfather silenced him, sounding suddenly sharp.

"On this quarterdeck, my lad, I'm still Captain. And I'll not be told by the crew what I may do. Not that I like the notion of pulling rank with you, boy. But there's a certain respect for the Captain's authority I'd like to see from you now and then. When I get it, maybe we can talk things over on a friendly basis."

Gene had flushed beneath his summer tan. "A river boat captain!" he said scornfully. "And you're not even that any more!"

With that he stamped about and hurled himself toward the stairs. Susan listened to his painful ascent, suffering for him and for his grandfather too. She was afraid to look at the Captain, and when he spoke, the cheerful note in his voice surprised her.

"That boy's got some growing up to do, I'm afraid. I apologize for him, Susan, since he doesn't know enough yet to apologize for himself."

"Don't you mind the way he talked to you?" she

asked in astonishment. "Aren't you angry with him?"

The Captain shook his head, and the feathery gray tufts at his temples waved gently with the movement. "What I am is sorry for him. When a man knows his own measure he doesn't talk like that about himself, or about other people. Gene's trouble is he doesn't like himself much right now. Till he gets a little self-respect, he's going to be mighty hard on everyone else. I don't aim to cater to him, but I don't aim to take what he says out on him either. There'll be a better way."

Susan heard him with a warm rush of liking. She wished she could do something to show her appreciation of his kindliness and generous understanding. Remembering Miss Altoona, she thought there might be a way to do him a favor.

"I should have told you before this," she said. "When I came up toward the house from that pool in the woods a little while ago, I saw somebody hiding under the upside-down tree in your back yard."

"Upside-down tree?" the Captain repeated, puzzled.

"That tree with all its branches growing toward the earth. I saw Miss Altoona Heath peeking out at your house through the branches as though she didn't want anyone to see her."

The Captain remained calm. "Altoona's getting as loony as a kite. Or maybe as foxy as a fox. But I don't think she's dangerous. At least not yet."

"What does she want?"

"That I can't tell you for sure. But there's one

thing certain—she's caught the same fever that's eating your Aunt Edith. My name for it is antique-itis. But exactly what it is she's laying for in this house, I don't know. I doubt if the whole kit and caboodle is worth more than a few thousand dollars combined. If your dad and Edith Sperry decide to buy the house—"

"Aunt Edith says if *you* decide to let us buy it," Susan corrected.

He smiled at her a little sadly. "There's that, of course. And my mind's not made up by a long shot. We'll hate to give it up. Gene especially. I know how the boy feels about those books. He's jealous of all the family history behind us. Right now he thinks it's all he has to be proud of. And he hates the idea of your folks coming in. He hates to give up one stick of furniture to anybody outside. That's the reason I'm taking things sort of slow. I don't want to do the wrong thing. We need the money, but it shouldn't be necessary to scrape the boy raw getting it. He has enough to worry about these days. Well, I guess I'll take my poster over to the firehouse and put it up on the front door. Gene's at home to hold the fort against Altoona."

Susan went upstairs with the Captain and found Gene sitting on the back steps staring at the tree that grew upside down.

"Got her trapped, haven't you?" Captain Dan said, sounding amused. "By the way, Susan, that tree is what we call a weeping beech. Good name, don't you think—the way it trails its branches down in a melancholy sort of way? Say—I wonder if you've been introduced to my grandson, Gene Foster? Gene, this young lady is Susan Price."

With that, the Captain carried his poster around to the front of the house and went off with it, not waiting to see how his grandson took the introduction.

Susan was almost afraid to look in Gene's direction. When she did, she found him looking at the weeping beech.

"Why didn't you tell me you were a Price?" he said crossly. "You didn't have to be sneaky about it."

Susan answered him as honestly as she could, though she had to swallow her indignation first. "I was afraid to tell you because you seemed so angry about the Prices coming to live in your house. I thought maybe we could get to be friends first, and then you wouldn't mind so much."

Gene started to answer, but at that moment Miss Altoona Heath must have tired of her cramped hiding place. She pushed the branches of the beech aside and let her entire plump body through the opening. The sunglasses were knocked askew on her nose in the process, and she adjusted them carefully and looked up at the sun as if to get her bearings. Then she walked casually away on her small, sandaled feet, without a backward glance for Gene or Susan or the house.

A nervous desire to giggle began to rise in Susan. She held it in until Miss Altoona was out of sight. Then it became too much for her. She dropped onto the top step beside Gene and began to laugh out loud. She put her face against her knees and laughed until the tears came. Gene stared at her for a startled moment and then he began to laugh with her, sounding uncertain at first. That set Susan off all the more, and in a moment the two were whooping with unrestrained laughter. As they sat there gurgling and choking, Mrs. Bancroft came out of the kitchen door and stared at them.

"What's so funny?" she demanded.

Susan and Gene stopped laughing and stared at each other.

"I—I don't know," Susan said. "It was that woman, I suppose. She looked so funny, and she was trying to be so—so calm. I do hope she didn't hear us laughing at her."

"I hope she didn't too," Mrs. Bancroft said. "The way she's been acting lately, I'd hate to have her angry with me."

"If she heard us, it serves her right," Gene said. "Snooping around the way she does. What do you suppose she's after?"

Mrs. Bancroft sniffed. "She's trying to dig up the family secret, if you ask me."

Gene sobered at once. "What are you talking about?"

Mrs. Bancroft came to the rail and shook out her dustcloth. "You needn't give me one of your black looks, young man. It's been common knowledge in this town ever since I can remember that there *is* a Teague secret. But you needn't worry about me giving it away. Long as I've worked here, I've seen nothing to set me shivering in the night. So I've nothing to talk about. It'll be lunch time soon. Better get washed up before your grandpa comes back."

At the mention of lunch, Susan sprang to her feet. "Oh dear! I promised Aunt Edith to be home in time for lunch. I'd better hurry. Good-bye, Gene."

She went down the steps and around toward the road in front of the house. A little to her surprise, Gene came with her.

At that moment the wild wail of a siren filled the air. It shrilled a single, rising cry and then died away. Susan felt Gene tense beside her.

"What's that?" she asked in alarm.

He relaxed quickly. "It's only the twelve o'clock siren. They blow it from the firehouse every day at this time to make sure it's working. Funny how that sound makes everyone jump. Grandfather says when it blows up for a real fire, every fireman tightens up inside, and the tension doesn't go away until they're all at work at the fire. I always feel it too."

"Have you ever gone to a fire with your grandfather?"

"Sure. When I'm home, he takes me along in his car. Sometimes I can help just sitting in his car. There's a spotlight I can work at night, and once I got to run the two-way radio."

He broke off suddenly, and Susan wondered if the things he had said to his grandfather had suddenly returned to his mind. He stared hard at the tree-tops as if he searched them for words. Then he plunged on doggedly.

"I shouldn't have said what I did to Grandfather.

He was a real captain, you know. And now he's chief of our fire company. That's a big honor. The men elect their chief by unanimous vote every year and there's never been a vote against Grandfather. I was a—a heel to say what I did."

Susan felt an unexpected surge of respect for this boy. Adam had taught her to admire courage, and although Gene could be prickly and unreasonable, he did have courage. That was what it took to admit he was wrong like this.

"I didn't pay any attention to what you said," Susan told him. "I don't think your grandfather did either. He knew you were angry and didn't mean what you were saying."

Gene would not accept that, however. "I meant some of what I said," he assured her. "But not about him."

He turned abruptly, without a good-bye, and disappeared around a corner of the Teague house. Susan stood for a moment looking after him in dismay. When they had laughed so companionably together, she had thought they were moving in the direction of being friends. But once more Gene Foster had made it quite clear that he did not mean to be friends with a Price. If he acted like this when Adam came, her brother would give him a hard time. Fortunately, Adam's coming was a long way off. Much could happen before then.

4

A Barrel of Books

THAT AFTERNOON Susan stayed in the shop to work with Aunt Edith. There were so many fascinating items in the big room that she knew it would take a long time to know them all. But it was fun to make a beginning.

She set to work dusting a tableful of small objects and she liked the task. There were butter molds in a tulip design, paperweights with snow scenes inside, and a sewing bird that clamped onto a table and would hold goods in its beak for a seamstress. She found a small, intricately fitted sewing case, and a few cold, bald darning eggs. A collection of pressed glass saucers was especially interesting. The patterns in the glass were beautiful and wonderfully varied. Aunt Edith said some of this old pressed glass had come from Sandwich on Cape Cod.

"How do you know when things are really old?" Susan puzzled.

"That's a good question. It takes a long time to become an expert. I think my fingers know more about antiques than my head does. Sometimes I can tell really old wood by the feel of the planes made by old-fashioned tools. Sometimes I can tell the sharpness of patterned glass better by touch than with my eye. Of course there are all sorts of signs. There should be worn places on the legs or rungs of old chairs. Or you can tell where a new screw has been inserted, or if drawer runners don't show proper wear."

"Do people ever make imitations of old things and try to sell them?"

"There's nothing wrong with making reproductions of old things if they're labeled for what they are," Aunt Edith said. "In fact, I have a table of just such items over there with a sign on it. That milk-colored glass dish with the sitting hen for a cover isn't the real thing. Sometimes a customer wants something inexpensive and doesn't care whether or not it's a true antique. So long as I play fair with him, it's all right to sell such things. But I've built up a reputation for good, sound stock, and that's something I value."

Aunt Edith went to wait on a customer who was looking for Victorian doorknobs. As Susan dusted one small object after another, she began to think about her strange morning. By now she wanted to talk to someone about all that had happened. When the customer had gone, Aunt Edith began to up-pack the big barrel of books from the Teague attic. As she worked, she listened while Susan told her some of the things that had happened after she had set off to find the Teague house. Especially about Gene.

"In order to understand what's happening to him

now," Aunt Edith said when she came to a break, "you have to understand a little about Gene's background. I can remember what an active boy he was when he was ten and eleven. He was good at all sorts of outdoor games, even at that age. His father had always been active in sports, and he was proud of Gene and took a lot of trouble teaching him what he knew. After his father's death, Gene and his mother came to live up here."

"It must have been terribly sad for Gene when his father died," Susan said.

"It was. Captain Foster had been wounded in the war, but he had recovered and he had a Purple Heart and all sorts of medals and service stripes. If he was a hero to his country, he was most of all a hero to his son. I think Gene is almost glad that his father can't see him the way he is now. For a while after the accident he gave up and wouldn't even try. But this summer, while his mother's away, he's alone with his grandfather and that's good for him. Though Captain Dan has his hands full, I'm afraid."

Before Aunt Edith could go on, two women parked their car in front of the shop and came inside. Aunt Edith smiled a greeting and let them wander about to suit themselves. But now she couldn't talk about Gene.

Susan finished her dusting and went over to watch her aunt pull dusty books out of the Teague barrel. Books of any sort always fascinated her. She even liked the smell of them and the crisp feeling of printed pages. These books, however, were some-

what less than crisp. There was an old copy of
Little Women in a green and gilt binding, its pages
yellowed with age. There was a worm-eaten, leather-
bound *Treasure Island*, with old-fashioned pictures.
There were some books by Washington Irving that
interested Aunt Edith, though she wasn't sure
whether they were first editions. There was also
a lot of what she termed "junk." Novels about an
imaginary kingdom called Graustark, books by
Harold Bell Wright and Gene Stratton Porter,
which Aunt Edith said weren't old enough to be
valuable.

The two women moved on about the shop,
touching everything that caught their attention,
picking things up and putting them down, whis-
pering to each other. At length they went out without buying anything, and Aunt Edith sighed.

"Lid lifters!" she said. "I knew they weren't really
interested. If only people wouldn't handle everything in the shop."

Now that they were alone again, Susan went on
with her story, telling her aunt about Miss Altoona's
further strange actions. And about what Mrs. Bancroft had said concerning the Teague family secret.

"What do you suppose she meant by that?" Susan
asked. "Is there really a secret?"

Aunt Edith pursed up her lips and blew the coat-
ing of dust off the edges of a book on English history.

"I wouldn't pay too much attention to Mrs. Bancroft," she warned. "A small town loves to gossip.
And of course the old-timers like best to gossip

about the newest people and the oldest people. Since the Teagues have been here longer than almost anybody else, their whole history has been picked apart and put together again year after year. Perhaps without very much relation to the truth. There have always been whisperings about the Teagues and some sort of secret."

"Do you think Miss Altoona is trying to find out the secret?"

"Of course I don't. I don't know anything about it. I think Altoona is developing a wild imagination, so goodness knows what she's after. Or what she thinks she's after. I do know that she begrudges me this barrel of books, though what she could hope to find in it I wouldn't know. I've come on nothing valuable so far."

Susan picked up the history book about the kings and queens of England and stared at it with growing interest. What sort of secret might a book contain? What sort of *valuable* secret? Aside, that is, from its printed contents, or its rareness as a collector's item. This book had no pictures, the print was painfully small and crowded on the page, and the lines were full of historical dates. It looked dull and she dropped it onto the pile beside Aunt Edith. Nevertheless, she remembered Gene's indignation over the way his grandfather had let Aunt Edith take the barrel, and so she looked carefully through the pages of every book in the pile. She wasn't sure what she expected to find, but nothing except a few brownish pressed flowers came to light, and an old bill for a pair of white kid gloves ordered

from a store in New York. No long-lost wills or
other secret papers fell out as she ruffled the pages.
The value, if any, must lie in the worth of the books
themselves, and so far Aunt Edith said she had not
found anything that would bring an impressive sum.

Her aunt made a last deep dip into the barrel
and brought out an old picture book with Kate
Greenaway illustrations.

"I'm almost sorry now that I didn't take Altoona
up on her ridiculous offer to buy the barrel without
even looking inside," she said. "Then I'd have been
able to pay the Captain more than these books
will bring otherwise. But, of course, I had to be
sure. Let's leave them out for now. Perhaps some
browser will see something among them he wants."

Susan leaned over the edge of the barrel, looking
into its dark depths. A thin sliver of white showed
in the bottom, and she wondered what it was. Since
it was not within her longest reach, she tipped the
barrel on its side and crawled into it.

"What on earth are you doing?" Aunt Edith
asked.

"I think there's something stuck in the bottom,"
Susan said, her voice echoing hollowly from inside.

Yes, she was right! There was still another book
at the very bottom. The sliver of white had been
the edge of its pages showing. The book was almost invisible because the cover was black and it
was of a large, oblong size that had caused it to be
wedged crosswise against the sides of the barrel.
It took a bit of prying to get it loose. When she had
it in her hands, she backed out of the barrel, sneez-

ing and blowing at the dust she had stirred up. Triumphantly she set the big flat book on a cherry wood table before her aunt.

"Maybe this is it!" she cried. "Maybe this old book has been stuck in that barrel for a hundred years and nobody knew it was there. Maybe *this* is the secret!"

Aunt Edith sighed. "And you with four practical-minded brothers in your family, Susan. What do they do about this imagination of yours?"

Susan paid no attention. The book had a stiff cover with leather reinforcements at the corners. There was no lettering on the outside, and it seemed to be some sort of ledger. She opened to the flyleaf, and Aunt Edith looked over her shoulder, her interest caught. Someone with an old-fashioned hand had written across the flyleaf in ink that might once have been black, but which had faded to a watery brown. The letters were difficult to make out but, after a moment of deciphering, Susan read the words aloud in a voice that had a quiver of excitement in it.

"Log of the Ship *Flying Sarah*, Rufus Teague, Captain."

"I apologize," Aunt Edith said softly. "I believe you *have* found something. Let me see—I think Rufus Teague would be Gene's great-great-great-grandfather. It was his son who built the house Captain Dan still lives in. Captain Rufus spent most of his life sailing around the world on clipper ships. In fact, the story goes that he died aboard this very *Flying Sarah*. I don't recall the details, but I believe something quite bloodcurdling and dramatic happened. I wonder if Captain Dan knows this book exists?"

"Do you think it's valuable?" Susan asked.

Aunt Edith nodded. "To Captain Dan and to Gene—yes. We must return it to them, of course. But probably it's of no great value in itself, though some collector of historical items might be willing to pay for it."

Aunt Edith took the old ship's log and put it out of the way on a high shelf, where it would be safe from customers until she had a chance to give it to Captain Dan. Susan noted its position thoughtfully. She meant to have a more careful look at the log, and perhaps read some of the notations in it. But for the moment she had been indoors long enough. Aunt Edith said by all means to run along and have fun, so Susan spent the rest of the afternoon exploring the other fork of the road that plunged down beside the gorge under the arched highway bridge. It led to the boat club docks at the very edge of the river. There motorboats and other small craft were moored in the enclosure near shore, and some of the owners were working on board, scrubbing decks or painting or doing other nautical chores. Two or three small boats were chugging noisily up and down the river.

Susan found herself a spot of shade under a willow tree and sat down on a big rock where she could watch the river traffic. The sun had grown hot in the afternoon sky and she felt comfortably lazy and disinclined to vigorous action.

It was a pleasant way to spend the hours and she was glad for once that Adam wasn't there to prod her into action. Adam was never happy unless he was stirring something up.

When she walked home again the katydids and cicadas in the woods were in full orchestra, but even their humming had a sleep-inducing effect. Boneless lay stretched on the steps of the Old Oak and she had to step over him to go inside. Aunt Edith was getting supper between waiting on customers, and Susan joined her in the living room—kitchen at the back.

"We had a visitor while you were away," her aunt said, slicing raw potatoes into a glass dish.

Susan turned on the water in the sink to wash her hands. "Was it Miss Altoona?" she asked.

"It was your friend Gene Foster," Aunt Edith said. "Will you hand me that carton of milk, please?"

Susan reached for the milk, not sure whether she was glad or sorry to have missed Gene. "What did he want?"

"Apparently he is still upset because his grandfather let those books out of the house. I assured him that there was nothing of any value in the lot, except for the old ship's log. I gave him that to return to his grandfather."

"Oh, you didn't!" Susan cried.

"Why shouldn't I?" Aunt Edith looked surprised. "You know we couldn't keep something that's probably of real value to the family."

"It isn't that—" Susan hesitated. "It's just that I was counting on looking through it first."

"I had a further look at it myself before Gene dropped in," Aunt Edith assured her. "And I found the going difficult. Mostly it was notations about longitude and latitude, about the weather, and about happenings aboard the ship. On one voyage the cook came down with the measles in mid-Pacific, and the first mate broke his arm during a typhoon. And there was information about cargoes, and that sort of thing. All this was probably important enough in its day but can hardly be interesting to us so many years later."

"Wasn't there anything else?" Susan asked.

"I didn't get all the way through," Aunt Edith admitted. "The book covered a number of voyages and it would take a long while to read through them all. Gene came in and I let him have the book."

"Was he pleased? Was he interested?"

"After a look or two he didn't seem to be. He thought the log would interest his grandfather, but he didn't get really excited about it himself. He seemed more interested in the other books I had unpacked from the barrel. I might have let him look through them if his manners had been a little better. He seemed to be implying that I had tried to cheat his grandfather out of something, and I couldn't feel very sympathetic. When he saw I wasn't going to turn the books over to him, he took the log and went off. I notice he's moving a little better these days, in spite of his brace."

Susan and her aunt had another cozy supper, with Boneless purring on the floor beside them.

Afterward, Aunt Edith had a visit to make, taking some books to a friend who was ill. She lighted the carriage lamps in the front windows of the shop and said Susan needn't bother locking the door—she would be right back, and this wasn't like New York City. There would be more air this hot night if the door was open.

When she had gone, Susan curled up in an easy chair in one corner of the shop, lighting a lamp of lacy Sandwich glass that had been adapted for electricity. She had reached an exciting place in the mystery she was reading and she wanted to find out what happened before she went to sleep tonight. In a day or two she would have to visit the library Aunt Edith had mentioned and take out a card. It always gave her an uncomfortable feeling to be running out of books to read.

The moon came up and glowed golden against the windows along one side of the house; a breeze stirred the leaves of the old oak tree from which the shop took its name, and whispered down the main aisle of the room. She was deeply lost in her story and miles away from Highland Crossing, following the speeding car in which the heroine was riding to the rescue of her younger brother. A sudden creaking on the far side of the room startled her so that her heart lurched and she almost dropped her book.

She sat up, shivering with the shock of surprise. The moon was just slipping behind a cloud, and the carriage lamps at the front of the shop could not illuminate the far corners, any more than did her nearby reading lamp. Here, hidden by the wide wings of her chair, she could not be seen from the main aisle of the shop. Nor could she see anything herself.

Cautiously, making no sound, she rose to her knees in the chair and peered around one wing to search the lighted areas and the shadows for anything that was amiss. Nothing stirred, and this time the sound hadn't been caused by Boneless, who was sleeping limply at her feet, her head turned up and a pink tongue visible. Probably the creaking had been nothing more than one of the sounds old buildings habitually make as their timbers cool after a hot summer day. Then, as her eyes studied the gloom, it seemed to her that there was, indeed, someone standing across the room, not far from the main aisle.

She steadied herself in the chair and held her breath as the moon came slowly out from behind its cloud and touched that section of the shop to life. Then she sighed in relief. The figure that had frightened her was only a marble boy on a pedestal —a cupid, with his bow raised, his small wings curving as if to take flight. She smiled at Boneless, who wakened and blinked at her with yellow eyes.

"Reading mystery stories makes me hear things," she told the cat.

The sound of her own voice was startling in the silence. As if in echo, something slapped on the floor across the shop with a small clatter. In an instant she knew with all her senses that there was someone there, and that whoever lurked among the tables and counters had been as startled by her presence as she was by his.

Plans that were a little wild flashed through her mind. Perhaps she should run to the rear of the shop, slam the door, lock it, and phone the police. But it was a long way, with a dozen unfamiliar objects in her path. The front door was ever farther and offered no escape, cut off as it was by the hidden intruder. Perhaps she should just start screaming in the hope that someone outside would hear and come to her rescue.

Then another course, more crafty, came to her. A way, perhaps, of frightening away whoever had come so stealthily into the shop.

"Aunt Edith!" she called sharply. "Aunt Edith, there's somebody in the shop. Maybe you'd better call the police!"

There was an instant of complete silence, as if the hidden one held his breath. Then a scornful voice spoke across the room.

"Don't be silly," it said. "I saw your aunt go off in her station wagon. There's nobody there to call. And I wouldn't hurt you anyway." The voice was Gene Foster's.

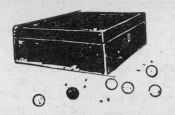

5

The Blackball Box

THE REACTION of relief left Susan all the more indignant over being frightened. She left her chair so abruptly that she stepped on Boneless' tail, and his yowling further unnerved her. By the time she crossed the room to where Gene was standing, she was really angry.

"Why did you sneak into the shop and scare me like that?" she cried.

Gene's face looked pale in the pale moonlight, but he stood his ground. "I wasn't trying to scare you. I didn't know you were around. And I'm not doing anything wrong. Those books"—he gestured toward the table—"belong to the Teagues. Grandfather didn't *give* them to Mrs. Sperry. He didn't even sell them to her. So they're still ours and I have a right to them if I like."

This was an odd way of figuring, and Susan didn't mean to accept it.

"Even if that's true," she said, "you still have no business sneaking into this shop to take something behind Aunt Edith's back."

"What are you going to do about it?" Gene asked defiantly.

Susan wasn't sure. Certainly Aunt Edith ought to know about this so she could decide how to handle it. Yet Susan hated to be the one to report what had happened. While she pondered the matter, they both heard the sound of the station wagon outside. A car door slammed, and a moment later Aunt Edith came briskly up the steps and into the shop. If she was surprised to find that Susan was not alone, she did not show it.

"Hello, Gene," she said cheerfully. "Was your grandfather pleased to have Rufus Teague's log turn up in that barrel?"

"I suppose he was glad to have it," Gene said grudgingly, and was silent.

Aunt Edith looked from him to Susan and back again. "It's fine that you dropped in for a visit," she told the boy. "I'm sure Susan will be glad of company. Let's go back to my living quarters. This is a good night for cold lemonade, and I think there are some oatmeal cookies around."

Susan released the breath she had been holding.

Perhaps everything would be all right after all, and Aunt Edith needn't know why Gene had come here. But Gene himself spoiled that notion.

"I didn't come for a visit," he said stiffly. "I came for those books. One of them, anyway. You wouldn't let me look at them this afternoon, so I came back after you went out in the car. After all, you left the door open."

He stood with both hands against a table, bracing himself in an upright position. His manner was far from friendly.

Aunt Edith looked at him in surprise. Then she said, "Let's have a little more light," and nodded to Susan, who ran quickly to the back of the shop and touched the switch that turned on the overhead lights. Gene blinked in the sudden glare, but his expression did not change. Susan wished she could shake him. His attitude would only make everything worse.

"Perhaps I don't quite understand," Aunt Edith said, sounding graver than before. "Are you telling me, Gene, that you waited until I left the shop and then came to get one of those books your grandfather put in my trust?"

"They're our books," Gene repeated stubbornly.

"Nevertheless, I'm responsible for them. If you wanted one, all you had to do was tell me which one and ask me pleasantly to let you take it back. I'd have been glad to, of course."

"You didn't say that this afternoon," Gene said.

Aunt Edith merely looked at him, and he had the grace to drop his eyes. He must have remembered that he had not behaved very well that afternoon.

"Anyway," he admitted, "I don't know which one. That's why I have to look through all of them."

"And if you had found the book you want, would you have taken it home without a word to either Susan or me?"

Gene repeated his formula doggedly. "They belong to us. I don't have to ask."

"If you'd like to look through the books now," Aunt Edith said, "go ahead. If you find the one you want, I'll let you have it. On one condition. When you take it home, I'd like you to tell your grandfather exactly how you got it and what happened here tonight. It's only right that he should know. I'm responsible for the books, and your grandfather is responsible—"

"He's not responsible for what I do!" Gene broke in hastily. "You can't blame him."

"I don't," Aunt Edith said gently. "And you're perfectly right. You are responsible for you. Nevertheless, this is something your grandfather should know, since I'm sure his main interest lies in helping you."

Gene made no move toward the books. His brooding gaze was fixed upon Aunt Edith, and he did not glance at Susan. She knew, however, that she was included in that black look. Now, more than ever, Gene would oppose having the Prices move into the Teague house. If only another house big enough could be found to solve their problem! But Aunt Edith had said there was little to be had in this area that would be both big and inexpensive.

Without another word, Gene turned away from the table of books. His gait was awkward again as he walked toward the door, as if he had forgotten how to use his crippled leg, as if the brace was hurting him. Aunt Edith let him go in silence, and perhaps he would have lurched down the steps and started off into the darkness alone, if a wailing sound had not pierced the night. It was the moan of a siren, spreading a cloak of frightening sound over Highland Crossing and along this part of the Hudson Valley. It was the same siren that sounded at twelve o'clock noon, but this was different. This sounded like the real thing.

Gene stopped in the doorway. "There's a fire!" he cried. "That's our siren, so it's right around here." Excitement had driven away the sullen defiance, and a new sort of anxiety possessed him.

As they listened, the sound moaned itself out, and for a few moments silence seemed to stun the entire area. Aunt Edith and Susan joined Gene on the front steps, and as they stood there the night seemed to blare into noisy life. There were voices calling, and the roar of car motors being started. Almost at once a car sped up the side road past the antique shop, moving toward the highway, and they heard the deeper roar of fire engines starting. All over town volunteer firemen must be dropping whatever they were doing to dash for the firehouse to get their instructions.

"If I'd been home, I could have gone with Grandfather!" Gene cried. "That was his car that just went by." He seemed beside himself with disappointment, the stack of books forgotten for the moment.

Susan glanced at her aunt and saw that the fire fever had seized her too. Already she was moving toward the station wagon.

"Close the shop door, Susan," she called. "Then come along, you two. Let's go find the fire. I wonder whose house it is?"

Surprisingly, Gene did not budge from the steps. "That's what people always do when there's a fire," he said sharply. "They block the roads and get in the way so the engines can't get through, and firemen can't do their work. It's especially bad up there on the hill where the roads are narrow."

Aunt Edith paused with her hand on the car door. "Of course you're right, Gene, and you're a credit to the chief when you speak up like that. We'd better be sensible and stay out of the way."

Across the highway and far up the hillside, a tongue of flame caught Susan's eye. "There it is!" she cried. "We can see it from here!"

Gene stared for a little while at the rising plume of flame, crackling red and yellow against the dark sky. Then he started slowly down the steps.

"Guess I'll get back home," he said.

Aunt Edith opened the car door. "Let us take you," she offered. "It's difficult walking in the dark, and there's no point in your making it on foot. But first—what about the suggestion I made a little while ago concerning the books?"

Gene shrugged with elaborate indifference. Quite

clearly he would not touch the books if the bargain required him to tell his grandfather what he had done. Moving stiff-legged on his brace, he started past the car, but Aunt Edith called him back.

"Wait a minute. I have a better idea. Let's all go over to the firehouse and see if we can do anything useful. You know how it is, Gene—when the firemen come back, hot coffee is what they need. Some of us who are free usually go over and help."

Gene's expression did not change, but when Aunt Edith gestured he slid into the front seat and Susan ran around the car and got in beside him, glad of this opportunity to take part in the excitement that was abroad tonight.

High on the hillside, flames soared brightly, but the fire engines were on the way and the night was noisy with the sound of cars scurrying off in the direction of the fire.

"I wonder whose house it is," Aunt Edith repeated as she started the motor. "I do hope the fire crew can put it out."

"If the alarm came in time, Grandfather will get it in hand," Gene said with confidence.

The station wagon turned onto the highway and they drove along the edge of the big lake Susan had noticed upon her arrival yesterday. Now its smooth surface shimmered in the moonlight, and across it she saw a large, square house with lights burning in several windows.

"That's Altoona Heath's house," Aunt Edith said. "I'll bet Altoona will join us at the firehouse before the evening's over. Now that there's no one around to tell her what she can't do, she's in on everything."

Gene made a snorting sound, expressing his disapproval of Altoona.

The firehouse itself was bright with lights, and there were several cars in the parking space at the back. Aunt Edith found a place for the station wagon, and they got out and approached the front steps.

"The original part, with the tower above it, used to be a schoolhouse," Aunt Edith explained to Susan. "It became too small for Highland Crossing, and we built a new school farther up the highway. Then, when Captain Dan got his volunteer company started, he persuaded the township to let the fire company take over this old schoolhouse. Since that time they've built on the wing at the right, which is big enough to house three engines, though at present we have only two."

The doors of the fire-engine section stood wide open, and the only person in sight was a man at a desk on telephone duty. A notice board over his head indicated the location of the fire.

Aunt Edith went over to read the notice and nodded. "Summer people. Careless, probably."

She led the way up a flight of steps to what used to be the schoolhouse door, and they stepped into a big meeting room, with game tables and small tables for dining set all about. In an adjacent kitchen several women were already at work.

"Captain Dan is proud of the fact that the company raises all its own funds for equipment and doesn't tax the property owners," Aunt Edith went on as they crossed the big room. "Everything is managed out of the income from meetings and parties held in this room, and of course from the big fair that's coming up pretty soon."

The kitchen buzzed with activity and talk. Sandwiches were being made as if for a picnic, and on the stove sat a huge old-fashioned coffeepot. Aunt Edith introduced Susan to several women and put a stack of bread before her to be buttered. Gene had promptly disappeared on pursuits of his own, perhaps not wanting to work with the women when he could not follow the men to the actual fire.

Rumor had it that someone had been smoking in bed at the Wilson place. That had started the fire, and it was hard to maneuver the engines up there on the hill. People ought to have better sense.

Someone next to Susan began to put pieces of cold ham between the slices of bread she was buttering, and she glanced up to see a plump woman with light-brown hair and round blue eyes working beside her. For a moment she did not recognize Miss Altoona. Without her sunglasses and peaked straw hat, she looked much less startling. Susan smiled at her uncertainly, not at all sure how she would respond. The blue eyes blinked at her, as if in surprise.

"You're Edith Sperry's niece, aren't you?" Miss Altoona asked. "How do you like Highland Crossing?"

Susan wasn't sure of the answer to that question. "Well—it's not exactly what I expected," she admitted. "I guess it's more exciting in some ways than I thought it would be."

"Oh?" said Miss Altoona, and then added with quick curiosity, "In what way is it more exciting?"

Susan hesitated. "This fire, for instance, and—and everything."

She didn't want to say that part of the excitement had to do with Altoona Heath herself, and, of course, with Gene Foster and his strange behavior over those books. Susan had expected a few weeks of sleepy quiet in a small town before school started. But somehow the people here didn't seem at all sleepy and quiet, and there was much more going on than she had dreamed there might be.

When enough sandwiches had been made and the women were sitting around talking, Susan slipped away and went in search of Gene. Exploring, she found a door that opened off the kitchen into a small hallway. Here a flight of crooked steps went steeply down to the fire-engine floor, and two other steps led upward into a big room over the engine-house. She chose the two steps up and walked through double doors to find Gene standing before a framed picture on the wall.

Quietly Susan went to stand beside him. The picture showed a group of smiling men in fire helmets, black coats, and boots. In the center of the group stood Captain Dan, looking a little younger than he did now.

"That was the very first company of volunteers," Gene said, and the pride in his voice was evident. "There weren't so many in the beginning. Now there are about forty regular volunteers in the company."

"Do they all go to every fire?" Susan asked.

"Most of them. Each man has a special post, of course. But since there's a rule that a man's business and his family has to come first in an emergency, there are substitutes for the most important posts. The way the men feel, it has to be something pretty important to keep any of them away."

Susan nodded toward the kitchen. "One of the women in there said this fire was up where the engines might have trouble getting to it. What does your grandfather do in a case like that?"

Gene seemed pleased to show his knowledge. "He'll get the engines in as close as possible and use the reels of extra hose. There're about three hundred feet of booster hose on each reel and two reels on each truck. And of course there's a pressure pump to increase the water pressure."

"But how can they get water way up there?"

"The fire's inside town limits, and water is piped all through the woods," he explained. "See the map on the wall over there? That shows every water outlet in the area this company serves. Every man has to know by heart where those outlets are. New volunteers attend classes right in this room to learn their job. And there're drills besides for everybody. In fact, when the siren up on the roof goes off, nobody but Grandfather knows for sure whether it's a real fire or a drill. He can order a drill any time he likes. Otherwise there might not be enough fires to keep the company in practice.

Do you want to see what it's like downstairs?"

Susan was pleased to be given a personally conducted tour. She followed as Gene started toward the stairs. But before he reached the door, he stopped and took a square mahogany box down from a shelf. The handsome wood had been polished to a glossy, dark-red shine.

"Do you know what this is?" he asked.

Susan did not, and Gene raised the lid of the box so she could look inside. The upper tray was filled with white marbles, among which a number of black ones rolled around.

"This is the way the men vote when a new volunteer wants to join the company," Gene explained. "Each of the regular volunteers reaches into this box and picks up one of those balls. Then he drops it through this slot at the front. When the balls are counted, if they are all white, the man's accepted. But if somebody drops a black ball through the slot, he's rejected. Look."

Gene picked up a few balls and dropped them into the opening. Then he pulled out a lower tray into which the balls had fallen. There were black balls among the white, and Susan could imagine how a man must feel to have that dark vote cast against him.

"They elect the chief every year like this, too," Gene said. "The next time will be at the end of the firemen's fair. That vote has to be unanimous, and Grandfather has never had a black ball cast against him."

"What if he did?"

"Then they'd have to pick out a new chief and keep voting and talking things over until one man was elected."

Gene put the box back on the shelf and led the way downstairs.

It seemed to Susan that now, while Gene was in this friendly mood, would be a good time for the question she had been wanting to ask. She paused on the zigzag of steps above him.

"Gene," she said softly, "why did you want to look through the books in that barrel?"

Gene stopped stock-still on the steps and looked up at her.

"So you're going to be a Miss Nosey!" he said. "But it won't do you any good. I won't tell you a thing."

"Then there really is a Teague secret?" Susan couldn't resist asking questions. "And those books have something to do with it!"

He turned his back on her and went down into the enginehouse. She barely caught the words he tossed over his shoulder.

"The books won't talk," he said.

Susan followed him into the big, empty engine room, and the man on duty at the desk looked up and smiled at them.

"Hi, Gene," he said. "How come you're not on duty in the chief's car?"

"I wasn't home when the alarm sounded," Gene said regretfully. He introduced Susan to the fireman, but he was much less friendly now, and she was sorry she had brought up the subject of the books.

The man at the desk seemed happy to point out various items of interest about the room for Susan's benefit. Over there on the wall was the switch that would set off the siren overhead—a switch that could also be thrown from the next town, in case help was needed there. And that wall phone was the direct connection with the firehouse up there. Sometimes the fire companies of several towns would respond to a really big fire. However, there wasn't much to see with the engines out, he explained, since most of the equipment was kept ready on the trucks and went right along with them.

Gene was the first to hear an engine returning from the hill above. "Get back in the corner," he told Susan. "Here they come!"

Sounding its siren, the first engine came down the highway, slowed, and made the turn, rolling into its exact position close to one wall of the room. Men in black hats, coats, and boots, like those in the picture Susan had seen, leaped down from the truck and began to get out of their things. Their boots were wet, and there was a smell of smoke about them. They were keyed up and full of talk about the fire. It hadn't been very bad, apparently. The alarm had been given in time and the damage was localized in one room. Though it was a wonder the man who had been smoking in bed had escaped with only minor burns. The chief had posted a watch to stay on and make sure there was no further outbreak of fire. As usual, sightseers had cluttered the scene, getting in the way and doing their best to get hurt.

Captain Dan himself—Chief Dan for tonight—came up in his own car a few moments later, and when he strode in, looking every inch in charge, Susan saw that his helmet was white, and easily distinguishable from those of the other men. In spite of his erect walk, however, he looked a little tired, and she wondered how he could keep up with such hard work when he was no longer young.

Wet hose had to be taken from the cribs and uncoiled to dry out. Axes and pike poles had to be cleaned, and every bit of equipment replaced in exact position so that it would be ready for the next alarm. But first the men took a break and went upstairs for coffee and sandwiches. This, it appeared, had been a fairly easy night. Sometimes, Susan gathered, it took hours and a lot of dangerous work to get a fire under control. Sometimes it was a losing battle, and the entire house burned down in spite of all they could do. In such a case, the big job was to prevent anything else from catching fire. Susan felt a little shivery listening to the stories.

Upstairs the atmosphere of excitement was heightened as the men came in. Even after the fire was over, it would take a while for everyone to relax and unwind. Gene seemed wound up too, even though he hadn't been at the fire, and he was full of technical questions that the men answered with good nature. Susan noted, however, that he took care to avoid his grandfather.

Then, while the women were cleaning up and about ready to leave, the fireman who had been on duty downstairs got up and spoke to the other men in a tone of voice that made everyone stop and look at him.

"You remember," he said, "that there was a matter we were all talking about last week, boys. Concerning a new honorary member of the company. How about settling it now with a regular vote?"

They seemed to know what he meant, and several smiled and nodded.

"Go bring us the box, will you, Gene?" the fireman said, and Gene, looking puzzled, went into the classroom and brought the mahogany box from its shelf. Susan could hear the marbles rolling around inside as he set it down on a table.

The bottom tray was emptied of marbles and the box made ready. Then, one by one, each man stepped up and chose a marble to drop through the slot. Though everyone stood around watching, no one could tell how a man voted, for his hand hid the color of the marble.

This time the chief voted last, and when the lower tray was pulled out it was clear that only white marbles had been dropped into it. The men applauded, and the spokesman held out his hand to Gene, who looked at him in surprise.

"You've just been voted into the company, Gene," the fireman said. "You are now official mascot and special assistant to the chief. We are proud to have you in the company, and we hope you will appreciate your post of honor and live up to the high standards of the Highland Crossing Fire Company."

Gene flushed a bright pink, but his eyes were alight with pleasure as he shook the fireman's hand.

"Speech! Speech!" someone shouted.

Gene said: "Th-thanks. Thanks an awful lot," and everyone applauded again.

Then the gathering began to break up. Susan, standing nearby, saw Captain Dan come over and shake his grandson's hand, and she couldn't help hearing what he said.

"The men figured this out themselves, and I'm proud they did. But where were you, boy, when the siren went off? I hollered up the stairs for you to come along, but you didn't answer."

Gene glanced across the room at Aunt Edith, but she wasn't looking his way. "I—I didn't hear you," he said, and his eyes did not meet his grandfather's.

That, Susan thought, was perfectly true, yet it was not the whole truth. She couldn't help wondering if Gene, who had just been elected to a position of honor in the fire company, would continue to hold back from his grandfather what had happened at the antique shop.

6

More About the Flying Sarah

IN THE DAYS after the fire, matters seemed to settle down to an uneasy quiet as far as Susan was concerned. The weather remained hot and clear. Sometimes a thunderstorm rumbled in the distance, but no rain fell in the immediate area. The summer people puttered around in their boats and cars, went fishing, had cookouts and swims, and now and then wandered into Aunt Edith's shop to see what was new. The paddlewheel day liner from New York came regularly to the dock below Bear Mountain, and visitors poured into the park and splashed about in the big swimming pool below the highway. August days were pleasant along the Hudson, but still Susan worried.

The news from home was about the same. Dad was a little better, but Mom wrote that he was pining for the Hudson River country where he had grown up. The doctors said he should be ready to get away from New York early in September, so it was important to have things settled with Captain Dan by that time. Besides, if the Price children were to start to new schools, the change ought to be at the beginning of the term.

But Captain Dan remained elusive, and nothing was settled.

One evening Susan drove with her aunt up a steep, winding hill that Aunt Edith said was the very road over which General Wayne—Mad Anthony Wayne—had marched his men in 1777 to attack Clinton's army. Up there in the dipping hills lay Doodletown, a very old village with a mixed history. Some people said that the words to "Yankee Doddle" had first been sung thereabouts, and that was how the town had got its name. But nobody knew whether that was really true.

On another evening, before it grew dark, they drove up the Storm King Highway, where there was a marvelous view of the Hudson country and West Point. But while these trips were interesting, Susan kept wondering about Gene Foster and his grandfather. What had happened after the fire? Was Gene still holding back the truth?

She saw the two of them only once, trudging along the road at Gene's pace, each carrying a fishing pole over his shoulder and a bait can in his hand. They were too far away for her to hail, and they did not see her. The sight reminded her of Adam, who loved to fish, though he hardly ever had a chance around New York.

The books from the Teague house were still stacked on the table where Aunt Edith had unpacked them, and so far none of them had been sold. On the day after the fire Susan went through them all carefully. Though nothing that shed any light on the mystery turned up, she noted one old book that was interesting because it had pictures all through of sailing ships. Turning the pages, she came upon a sketch of the *Flying Sarah*, Captain Rufus Teague's ship. Apparently he had been both owner and captain of the ship on which he had met with violent death. The sketch showed considerable detail of the ship, from her figurehead at the prow to the great iron anchor at the stern. The artist had drawn a full-rigged ship, with every sail set, so that it made a stirring and dramatic sight. "How beautiful those old clipper ships must have been!" Susan thought. Something had been lost with the coming of steam and funnels.

When she showed the picture to Aunt Edith, her aunt said that this book, too, must be returned to Captain Dan.

One Saturday afternoon Susan set off for the little library, with Aunt Edith's card to use until she could get one of her own. While Highland Crossing had no real main street, as larger towns did, there was a block of small stores cutting off in a diagonal on the other side of the highway and the volunteer library was located in this block.

The post office was here, and a drugstore. There was also a fascinating, old-fashioned country store that carried everything from dresses to garden implements. And here, in a wedge of space beside the post office, was the library.

Since the hour was just past two o'clock, the door stood open, and Susan went up the steps and inside to have her first look around. The single room was small and L-shaped, with shelves that volunteer workers had built along the walls. Susan's first impression was a pleasant one of cheerfulness. The donated furniture had been repainted. A bright-red geranium grew in a pot on a table where magazines lay spread. A cork bulletin board displayed the jackets of several new books, and on the walls were interesting pictures loaned by people in the town.

Pleased with all she saw, Susan turned toward the librarian's desk off to one side of the door and stared in surprise. The librarian on duty this afternoon was Miss Altoona Heath.

At the moment she was waiting on a rather young book borrower—a little girl about eight years old. Several books were spread out on the desk before her, and Miss Altoona was studying them with an air of such despairing concentration that she did not notice Susan.

"I'm sorry," Miss Altoona said to the questioning young lady, "but I really don't know which one is the best. And I don't know if any of them is about a haunted house."

Susan stepped closer to the desk and glanced at the assorted titles. She had read four of these books when she was younger, and she reached without hesitation for her favorite.

"This one is very good," she assured the little girl. "Maybe it's not about a haunted house, but I think you'll like it. And this one's good too. It's the story of a girl from an orphanage who thought she wasn't going to like the outside world. I cried like anything when I read it."

The child's face brightened. "I love a story that makes me cry," she said. "May I have these two, please?"

Miss Altoona sighed in relief and stamped the book cards. "I didn't realize when I volunteered for Saturday afternoons that I'd be expected to help with children's books too. So far there have been more children coming in than grown-ups. I don't know what I'm going to do."

"You could read some of the books," Susan suggested.

Miss Altoona's round, blue eyes widened still more.

"Read them?" she repeated blankly, as if this was an unheard-of idea. "*Children's* books?"

"Maybe you'd like them," Susan said. "If you want, I can pick out a few I know are good and you could take them home to read."

"M-m," said Miss Altoona doubtfully. "Maybe I could, at that. Most anything would be better than some of the television shows I've been watching lately. All right—go ahead and pick some out for me."

The request was made grudgingly, but as Susan went to work searching the shelves of young peoples' books for something she had not read, she watched for books to recommend to Miss Altoona as well.

When she had gathered a few books together, she took them to the desk so Miss Altoona might copy down authors and titles. Then Susan filled out the form that would bring her a card of her own, while Miss Altoona watched her—a little like a cat watching a mouse. That steady, blue gaze made Susan faintly uncomfortable, and she felt she would be glad to get away from the library. However, just as she picked up her books to leave, Miss Altoona spoke to her abruptly.

"I've been meaning to come over and have a look at those books your aunt wheedled out of Captain Dan, she said.

"She didn't *wheedle* them," Susan said quickly. "They weren't doing any good up there in the Captain's attic, and Aunt Edith thought they might bring him some money."

Miss Altoona listened as though she did not believe a word of this. "And do you think they will?"

"I'm afraid not," Susan admitted. "Mostly they're just old novels and books Aunt Edith says aren't worth anything. Though I found one book about clipper ships with a picture of the *Flying Sarah* in it, so we'll give that one back to the Captain."

"The *Flying Sarah?*" Miss Altoona leaned forward with her elbows on the desk, a gleam of interest in her eyes. "Maybe that's the one! The *Flying Sarah* was the ship of which old Rufus Teague was captain."

Susan nodded. "That's right. But what do you mean—'that's the one'? Why are you interested in those old books?"

Miss Altoona blinked once or twice and veered away from the question, her expression guarded. "I understand you and your family may be moving into the Captain's house one of these days."

"We hope to," Susan said.

"I suppose you realize," said Miss Altoona, "that the Teague house is haunted?"

Susan stared at her. She was beginning to wonder if Miss Altoona might be just a little crazy. It was not a pleasant thought, and she began to edge her way toward the door.

The woman went on, not looking at Susan now, speaking almost as if to herself. "People say old Sarah Teague comes back sometimes. From what I've heard, it sounds like what she would do. She was supposed to be pretty strong-minded in her day. I've heard my grandfather tell stories about the Teagues. Rufus named his favorite ship after her because he claimed anything that bore her name could sail any sea. But the name didn't protect him in the end, because he was murdered aboard his own ship. Afterward, they say, Sarah took charge of all his business and ran the shipping company herself."

In spite of her desire to get away, Susan had to ask one more question. "But why do you think Sarah Teague comes back to—to—"

"To haunt the house?" Miss Altoona supplied readily, looking as if she had begun to enjoy her own ghost story. "Why, because she died tragically too—right on the grounds of the house. She was drowned in that little pond in the woods nearby."

A shiver ran unsuppressed through Susan. Only a few days ago she had stood upon a log in that pond, looking into the water, sensing the strange mystery that seemed to hover about the place. Was it possible, she wondered, for a terrible tragedy to set its stamp upon the surroundings where it had happened?

Miss Altoona smiled gently to herself as if she was pleased at whatever she had accomplished. Perhaps, Susan thought, the woman was trying to frighten her. Though she couldn't see why. The thought banished her shivers, and she spoke up more boldly.

"The first time I went to the Teague house, I saw *you* haunting it," she told her.

Miss Altoona turned faintly pink, and her eyes did not meet Susan's. "I really had a good plan that day, but it didn't work out. I was waiting for Gene and his grandfather to leave the house so I could knock on the front door. When Mrs. Bancroft came, I meant to say I was there to call on the Captain and would wait until he returned. Mrs. Bancroft would have invited me into the living room, and probably she'd have left me there. Unfortunately, Gene didn't leave and you turned up, so my plan didn't work out very well."

"But why did you want to be alone in the Captain's living rooms?"

A secretive, cautious look came over Miss Altoona's face, and Susan knew she had pushed her questions too far.

"If I told you," the woman said, "it might spoil everything. After all, *I* want to find it first."

It would be no use, Susan was sure, to try her with another question. Miss Altoona's mouth was pursed into a round pout, as if a small bag had been neatly gathered to keep any more of its contents from spilling out. Anyway, Susan had heard enough for one day. She wanted to get outside into the fresh air and away from the strange Miss Altoona Heath.

She picked up her books and said a hasty goodbye as she hurried out the library door. Of all the unbelievable things with which she had been confronted this afternoon, Miss Altoona herself seemed the most fantastic of all.

When she came within sight of Aunt Edith's shop, she was in time to see Captain Dan climbing the front steps. Cene Foster, looking stiff and a little frightened, was clumping after him.

Susan began to run. Something was about to happen that she didn't want to miss.

7

The Forbidden Rock

SUSAN FOLLOWED the walk to the Old Oak on the run and dashed up the steps. She had never seen the Captain looking so stern, or Gene so chastened.

Aunt Edith had just finished with a customer, and she came to greet the Captain as he entered the door.

"Good afternoon, Captain Dan. It's good to see you. You don't visit us often enough. Hello, Gene."

Gene's "hello" was subdued, and he did not look at Susan as she slipped through the door behind him.

"I'm sorry, Edith," Captain Dan said, "but this isn't a social call. This grandson of mine has told me what he did here one night. That he sneaked into your shop meaning to take a book behind your back."

Aunt Edith smiled, without rancor, at Gene. "I had a feeling he would tell you. And, of course, as Gene says, he feels that the books are really yours, and therefore he wouldn't have been taking anything that belonged to me."

The Captain looked sternly at his grandson. "And what have you to say about this?"

Gene raised his chin in a proud sort of way. "Everything Mrs. Sperry says is true. Just the same, I know I had no business getting one of those books behind her back. But I didn't want her to know what I was looking for."

"You may look all you like now," Aunt Edith said.

Before Gene could speak, Captain Dan shook his head. "Never mind the books. Under the circumstances, I don't think he's earned a look at them. You've a good head on your shoulders, Gene, and you can figure things out better than this. We'll get along now, boy."

Gene hesitated. "But Grandfather, you know why I want to find the book."

"I know why," Captain Dan said, "but I don't think it matters. If there is one, let it keep its secret. It's not important to us. I'd rather get a few dollars for the lot, if that's possible."

He said good-bye, and Gene followed him reluctantly out of the shop. When they had gone, Aunt Edith stared at Susan in bewilderment.

"Now what was that all about?" she asked.

"I think it's about the Teague secret," Susan said. "Miss Altoona was the volunteer librarian this afternoon, so I got to talk to her. She's looking for something in that house, and one of these books may have something to do with it. She tried to tell me that the house is haunted. I think she wanted to frighten me."

"What *can* the woman be up to?" Aunt Edith said, "Though, of course, in a sense it is haunted. Every old house is haunted. And ought to be. Haunted by memories of the people who lived and died there, and the things that happened within its walls. An old house has to know death as well as life, Susan. The sad thing would be an old house that wasn't haunted because there was no one left to remember those who had gone before, or to tell stories about them."

Idly Susan picked up a small cup and saucer—very delicate and eggshell-fine, with tiny painted rosebuds across the china. Studying it, she thought of what her aunt meant. Someone long ago had used this cup and saucer. Yet those who had held it in their hands were gone, and no one who looked at the little cup knew or cared about them. Yes—a house that was haunted in the way Aunt Edith said must be a more fortunate place than one whose memories, both tragic and happy, had been altogether forgotten. But she still felt that Miss Altoona had not meant this when she spoke about haunting.

"Do you think—" Susan began, and then hesitated, trying to soften her words. "Do you think Miss Altoona might be—well—a little bit crazy?"

"Goodness, no!" Aunt Edith said quickly. "No more than the rest of us. Odd, perhaps, but not one bit crazy."

Susan nodded thoughtfully. She did not feel altogether reassured. An unbalanced Altoona might be pardoned for her strange ways, but one who was completely sane and behaved the way she did might well be a dangerous person. Dangerous because she was after something, because she knew quite well what she was doing, and meant to go ahead, no matter what.

Someone came into the shop at this moment, looking for Early American samplers, and Aunt Edith opened a drawer to take out her collection of embroidered mottoes.

"I think I'll go out for a while," Susan said, and her aunt nodded and waved a hand.

Outside Susan took the downhill road, thinking about many things as she followed it. She was glad Gene had owned up to what he had done, instead of trying to keep it from his grandfather. There was really so much to like about Gene, if she could only get past his prickly defense. Even at her first meeting with him, when her main concern was to make friends because of the house and all it meant to her family, she had still been drawn to the boy himself. His unhappy plight, and the courage he could show at times in his attempt to deal with it, weighed against the unpleasant facets of his character.

Was the book with the sailing-ship pictures the one Gene had wanted, as Miss Altoona seemed to think? Aunt Edith had forgotten to give it to the Captain. It might be interesting to look more carefully through that book and see what might be discovered in it. Then, Susan decided, she would give it to Gene herself and perhaps be able to please him in that small way. Regardless of what his grandfather had said, she felt he deserved the book now.

When she came to the fork in the road, Susan chose the left-hand branch and walked along, watching for the path that wound down through the woods to the place where she had come upon Gene that first day. She still wanted to climb the big rock he had been so unpleasant about, and if he had gone home with his grandfather, this was her chance. After all, he couldn't keep people out of unfenced woods.

She walked lazily along, in no hurry now. In an open place she came upon a clump of goldenrod, a deeper yellow than the sunlight. A dragonfly hovered before her, its transparent wings flickering in the sun before it darted away. In the woods the cicadas kept up their continuous hum, and a little farther along, one of them lay on its back in the path, waving its legs futilely in the air. Susan bent to turn the little brown creature gently with a twig before she went on her way.

The peace of the afternoon was suddenly shattered by a staccato sound that came sharply to her ears. It was a rapid tattoo that she could not identify. By now she knew the distant crackle of rifle fire from the West Point range, but this was something much closer—a volley of quick, beating sounds, a pause, then a sharp repetition of the volley, followed at length by the humming quiet of the woods. She was reminded of the time she had come upon Gene playing with his basketball. But this sound was nothing like that, and though she listened, it was not repeated.

The path dipped into the flat clearing where the great rock raised its castle ramparts above the Hudson. Gene's improvised basket held out its iron hoop for the next ball to be dropped through it, but no dark-browed boy stood guard at its foot. The rock mountain was hers if she wanted it.

Once more she took a running start and went several feet up the rough wall of rock. Then, clinging to crevices with her fingers, while her feet sought for firm ledges, she inched her way up the slanting side to the very top. Here the rock flattened out, and the view, as she had expected, was breathtaking.

To her right, Bear Mountain Bridge shone in the sun as though it were made of silver threads, riding the lines of its suspension wires from this western shore across the river. The hill called Anthony's Nose rose in a sharp, rugged cliff on the far side. Between the two banks the Hudson seemed to flow without a ripple to mar its surface, and what boats were in view moved languidly upon smooth glass. As she watched, a glittering modern train snaked along the opposite bank, sounding the mooing horn that had replaced the old-fashioned whistle.

Susan watched it out of sight, filled with a sense of that freedom which heights always gave her. Then she turned to examine the fortification of rock more carefully, wondering why Gene had not wanted her to climb it. Near the edge on one side a sharp slab broke the plane, protruding like a jagged tooth. There seemed to be some sort of marking on its face, and Susan bent to examine it more closely. To her surprise, she saw that someone had chiseled letters—words—into the very rock. The markings were blurred and weathered as if they had been made a long time ago, and the letters wavered as though cut by a hand that was not very sure of itself. Nevertheless, she could read what it said:

G.F.
HIS ROCK

The initials, of course, stood for "Gene Foster." Clearly he had claimed this rock as an explorer might claim a peak he was the first to stand upon. But the Gene Foster of the crippled leg could never have climbed this rock. So it had been climbed by a much younger Gene—a little boy playing at make-believe, triumphantly reaching the peak of his mountain and claiming it forever.

Susan touched the weatherworn letters sadly. She knew now why Gene had not wanted her to climb the rock. He must have experienced a rush of indignant feeling when he saw an upstart stranger —and a girl, at that, but with two good legs so that she could go where he could not—climbing this rock which he had once felt was his. She understood and she would not come up here again. Not even if Gene wasn't here to see her.

The sudden clatter of staccato sound that she had heard before reached her again. It was nearer now, and seemed to come from beyond the far side of the rock. Gingerly Susan went to the edge and looked down. She found that she was peering almost directly into a stone chimney that rose at one end of a little cabin with a slanting roof. Some of the gray shingles had been patched, but the roof looked neat and weather-sound, and what she could see of the walls of the cabin were painted a clean forest green. From beyond the cabin came the beating sound that she could not identify.

There was someone down there, out of sight, and she had a feeling it was Gene. He had not gone home with his grandfather, after all, but had come to this place for some purpose of his own. He mustn't discover that she had violated his private castle by climbing it behind his back. Quickly she returned to the side she had come up and went down backward, finding the descent more difficult than the ascent, afraid every moment that Gene would come around the foot of the rock and discover her before she was down.

Nothing happened, however, and between the sharp bursts of sound there were stretches of silence. When she was safely back to level ground, she rounded the great mound of rock and found a path cutting down toward the little cabin. She couldn't see the cabin itself now, but there was a spring nearby, which made this an especially suitable place for someone to live. Water trickled beneath the path under a small, homemade culvert.

Susan stepped across it and came into full view of the cabin just as the rattle of sound began again. She saw what it was and stood still in surprise. A lean-to porch had been built along the front of the cabin, and from its roof hung a leather bag. Gene, his legs braced for balance, stood before this bag with his fists raised. His face was flushed from the effort he had been making. As Susan stared, he raised his fists and set the punching bag rocking with a rapid series of blows.

When he paused for a rest, Susan stepped into view. "You're awfully good at that," she told him. "Is it very hard to do?"

He looked at her in evident exasperation. "I never saw anybody who could keep popping up the way you do," he said.

Adam often said things like that, and Susan didn't really mind. After all, she had to be somewhere, and part of the time that somewhere would be where other people were, whether they liked it or not.

"Will you let me try?" she asked.

That seemed to amuse him, and he stepped back from the bag.

"Go ahead," he told her.

She lifted an uncertain fist and tapped the bag gently. It hardly stirred, so the next thump she gave it was a good one. The bag flew sharply up against the roof and just as sharply back against the side of her head.

"Ouch!" Susan cried, and sat down on the porch

floor without grace or ceremony. It was her turn to frown. "Why didn't you tell me it would do that?" she demanded.

"You didn't ask me," Gene said.

At least he wasn't laughing out loud at her, as she knew Adam would have done, though there was something suspiciously like a twinkle in his eyes.

"You aren't hurt, are you?" he added.

She was stinging a little in several places, but she had to admit that her feelings and dignity were hurt more than anything else. Resolutely she stood up to the bag and raised her fists before her face as if it might attack her of its own free will.

"Show me how," she said.

With surprising patience and without sarcasm, Gene tried his best to show her how to punch the bag. It wasn't his fault, Susan had to admit, that the lesson was not successful. She was afraid of the bag now and reluctant to give it a good blow. Besides, the whole thing was more complicated than she had expected. After a few tries she gave up rather meekly. It seemed a most unrewarding sport.

"Why do you want to punch an old bag like that anyway?" she asked.

Gene answered without evasion. "Because Grandfather said I was getting puny and spoiled and helpless. Because he was right about my muscles turning into old rubber, and because this is hard to do when you can't balance properly."

"You're a lot like my brother Adam," she told

him, nodding her understanding. "Adam likes to do things that are hard. I think you'll like Adam when he comes up here next month."

All friendliness went out of him, and he regarded her coldly. "What good would it do me to like your brother? He wouldn't like me." Gene turned his back on her and opened the door of the cabin. In a moment, she knew, he would go inside and leave her standing here on the porch, dismissed.

"That's the silliest thing I ever heard in my whole life!" she said sharply. "Why shouldn't Adam like you if you were ready to like him?"

Gene stepped through the door. "Who said I'd like him? If you can't figure it out, wait and see," he said, and shut the door in her face.

His action was rude and bad-tempered, but with four brothers she had been treated to rude bad tempers before this. It did not bother her especially.

Perhaps she ought to write Adam a letter about Gene Foster and prepare him a little. Adam was apt to act quickly and think later. But if someone took the trouble to explain things to him, he might be more favorably inclined toward Gene and more apt to be patient in the face of Gene's own difficult personality. Yes, that was exactly what she would do.

Having come to a decision, she stepped down the single step from the porch and stood for a moment longer looking at the neat green cabin. It was spic and span with fresh paint, and in good repair. The broad stone chimney at one end indicated a wide fireplace that would make for comfort inside. But livable though it seemed, the cabin was a far cry from the many-roomed house where Captain Dan had lived all his life. She wondered how he and Gene would get used to a place so tiny. That thought brought her back to the question of whether they would be willing to get used to it.

She had made very little progress with Gene, and if the Captain continued reluctant to hurt him by this move, the Prices might find themselves unable to do what was so important to Dad and thus to the rest of the family as well.

She had reached a state of discouragement by the time she climbed the hill and returned to the shop. She went back to Aunt Edith's quarters and found her aunt hanging up the phone.

"Oh dear!" Aunt Edith said. "If you had come in two seconds sooner you could have talked to your mother. She sent you her love and said she could hardly wait to see you."

The disappointment was keen, but Aunt Edith said perhaps she would be interested in a possible change in plans that her mother had called about. A change that might put immediate pressure upon Captain Dan and pry him into a decision.

"Adam's coming up," Aunt Edith said. "Your father is better and your mother feels she can spare Adam. So he wants to come up here next week."

For a moment Susan's eyes brightened at the thought of seeing Adam sooner than she had expected. Then she looked discouraged again.

"What if Captain Dan says no?" she asked.

"Whether he decides to sell the house or not, he can at least rent it to us," Aunt Edith said firmly. "If he'll permit it, we'll move in right away so that Adam can join us."

This sounded wonderful, but Susan still felt doubtful.

"Let me see," Aunt Edith pondered. "Tomorrow is Sunday. We'll leave for church a little early and stop in to see Captain Dan. Before church is a good time to catch him. After all, his house is so big that there would be no need for them to move out at once, even if we moved in. They could go right on occupying their own rooms until it was convenient for them to move out."

Susan nodded thoughtfully. Aunt Edith could be very persuasive, and Captain Dan himself had admitted that it was hard to stand up to her. This might work out after all. But what about the long-run prospects which were so important? What would happen when Adam and Gene were thrown together so suddenly, without preparation ahead of time? There would be no time now to let Adam know the details about Gene, or to gain his patience and cooperation.

Clearly there were problems coming up in the immediate future, and she wasn't at all sure they could be easily solved.

8

A Change of Plans

"You look very nice, my dear," Aunt Edith said when Susan came downstairs ready for church the next morning.

She had put on her pale-blue cotton and Dacron, with the full skirt of unpressed pleats that stood out in a swirl over her petticoat. Her shoes were white flats with frivolous blue bows on each toe, and because this was Sunday, she had put on her hat and white gloves. Oddly enough, it felt very nice to be out of jeans this morning.

Aunt Edith wore a trim gray cotton suit and a small white hat that revealed a wing of her gray hair underneath its brim.

The church was only a short distance down the highway, but since they meant to go down to see Captain Dan, Aunt Edith decided to take the station wagon. When they drove up, Captain Dan was sitting on the veranda, dressed up in a slightly shiny blue suit. He rose to greet them when Aunt Edith parked and they got out of the car.

"I wonder if we could talk to you for a few moments?" Aunt Edith said. "Then perhaps we can give you a lift to church."

101

"I'm at your service, ladies," the Captain said, sounding a little formal, as if he had put on special Sunday manners along with his suit. "And we'll accept the lift and thank you for it. Suppose we go inside where the chairs are more comfortable."

Susan was glad to get a better look at the big living room of the Teague house. Again she was impressed by both its size and its air of dignified gloom. The front windows were shaded by the porch roof, and what other windows there were did not seem very large, so not much light filtered into its depths. The dark-red mahogany panels seemed to add to the gloom, and the branching stairway at the back, leading to the open balcony and the second-floor rooms above, seemed lost in even deeper shadow.

For some reason Miss Altoona's words returned to Susan's mind. "I want to find it first," she had said. What was she searching for and where was it hidden?

Captain Dan switched on an old-fashioned floor lamp with a fringed shade and invited Susan and Aunt Edith to sit down. Before the cold hearth with its heavy brass andirons lay a great bear rug, as dusky in its color as the rest of the room.

Gene was nowhere in sight, and Susan wished he would appear, since she wanted to know his reaction to the request Aunt Edith meant to make. Not that she couldn't guess what it would be.

Her aunt came to the point at once, explaining about the phone call from New York and the fact that Adam would arrive on Tuesday. She spoke as if there were no doubts at all in her mind about the Captain's letting them have the house.

"If it won't inconvenience you too much," she went on, "Susan and I would like to move in—at least with some of our things—as soon as we can. Then we'll be settled for at least a day or two before Adam arrives."

The Captain stared into the empty fireplace for a long moment. He looked thoroughly cornered and uncomfortable.

"When would you like to come?" he asked.

"Any time you say we may," Aunt Edith said. "But it shouldn't be necessary for you and Gene to move out at such short notice. I'm sure the three of us can keep out of your way and not inconvenience you too much in a house as big as this."

"I know I've kept you waiting too long for a decision," the Captain said softly. "But I'd like to talk it over once more with Gene. The boy is concerned too, and—"

A voice from the stair landing broke in upon his words. "I heard, Grandfather. I was just coming downstairs."

Moving with his stiff-legged gait, Gene descended the last steps and stood facing them in the living room. After a brief "good morning," he spoke directly to his grandfather.

"If Mrs. Sperry is going to move in, let's go down to the cabin right away," he urged. "A lot of our things are down there already, and I can get the rest of what I want packed this afternoon."

His voice sounded stiff and a little strained. He was not happy about the change in plans, but it was clear that he did not want to remain if she and Aunt Edith were moving into the house.

His grandfather smiled at him and turned to Susan's aunt. "It's settled then. You can come in today, if you like. On a rental basis. I still don't know whether we want to sell or not."

Aunt Edith did a quick calculation in her head.

"That will be fine. Susan can help me with our packing. Then we can sleep here tonight and begin to get settled in the morning. Since the shop's closed on Mondays, this is a good opportunity. Thank you both for agreeing to this."

Gene did not look as though he wanted to be thanked, and when they all went outside and got into the station wagon, he remained silent, not joining in the talk between Aunt Edith and his grandfather. Susan sat beside him in the back seat and tried uneasily to make conversation.

"I wish you were staying in the house so you could meet Adam right away," she said. She was not sure her words were true, but she wanted to say them anyway.

Gene answered shortly. "If we have to go, it's better to go quickly. It's better not to think about it."

"But you'll come up to visit us soon, won't you?" Susan asked. "We'll want you to come."

"I don't want to come," he said, and did not speak again until the station wagon pulled up before the church he and his grandfather attended.

The Captain declined Aunt Edith's offer to stop by and take them home. It was only a short walk, and they could make it on foot.

Aunt Edith drove on and found a place to park near her own church, not far away.

Susan enjoyed the feeling of being in a small-town church. The morning light glowed through the jeweled colors of a tall stained-glass window, and there was a feeling of quiet peace beneath the vaulted arches of the roof. Somehow she had the same sort of feeling here that she felt at times out beneath trees, with the sky showing through.

Afterward, when they drove back along the highway toward the shop, they came upon Altoona Heath walking home. The flowered pattern of her print dress was large and rather bright, so that she stood out among the others who followed the edge of the road. Aunt Edith drew the car up beside her and leaned across Susan.

"Good morning, Altoona. May we give you a ride home?"

Miss Altoona accepted with evident pleasure and got into the front seat beside Susan, overflowing into a little more than her share of the space. She was hardly settled before she began to ask questions.

"When do you expect to move into the Teague house, Edith?"

"We're moving in tonight," Aunt Edith told her, turning the car off the main highway to follow the lake around to Miss Altoona's place on the far side.

"So soon!" Miss Altoona cried. "Old Sarah must be turning in her grave!"

"Sarah? Oh, you mean Rufus Teague's wife? I don't imagine she is," Aunt Edith said calmly. "Our ancestors had enough troubles of their own without worrying about ours."

"I wouldn't be so sure," Miss Altoona said. "I suppose you know the story of how she threatened to return and haunt her own house if things didn't go the way she wanted them to? Having her own flesh and blood move out can't be what she wants."

Aunt Edith's tone was dry and a little disapproving. "I've heard the story, but I can't say I put much stock in it."

"Well, *I* put stock in it," said Miss Altoona. "I'd watch out if I were in your shoes, moving in there with all Sarah's old things and knowing how much she must hate it."

The station wagon came to a halt before the elaborate house that Oscar Heath had built in the great days of his wealth.

"Here you are," Aunt Edith said, cheerfully.

Miss Altoona gave Susan a doubtful smile and got out of the car. Then she hesitated, her hand on the door. "Would you care to come in?" she asked, somewhat awkwardly.

Aunt Edith shook her head. "Thanks, but we'd better not take the time now. Susan and I have a dozen chores waiting for us."

When Susan looked back as they drove away, she saw that Miss Altoona had stayed where she was on the walk, staring after them.

Through the rest of the day, however, she and her aunt were so busy that she had little time to think about Miss Altoona and her odd behavior.

Right after supper she and her aunt took their suitcases and a basketful of odds and ends up to the Teague house to move in for their first night.

Mrs. Bancroft came to let them in, explaining that Captain Dan and Gene had gone down to the cabin that afternoon.

"Captain has kept the extra key," she informed Aunt Edith. "He said to tell you he may be in and out for a few days until he gets everything he wants. He hopes you won't mind."

"Of course we won't," Aunt Edith said. "Let's take our things upstairs, Susan. Are there any particular rooms you'd like us to take?"

"I've got everything clean and made up," Mrs. Bancroft said, "so it's no matter to me. There're bedrooms on both the second and third floor. You can pick what you like. I have my own room downstairs at the back."

Susan and her aunt followed Mrs. Bancroft up the main stairway, lighted now by a chandelier that banished shadows to the far corners of the great room below.

"The room I'd like is here on the second floor," Aunt Edith said. "It's at the side, with a little sitting room adjoining While I have a look, you see where you would like to be, Susan."

Susan glanced uncertainly about the narrow balcony that overlooked the living room. Aunt Edith's room was on a hallway opening from the balcony. Down this hall a smaller staircase led to the third floor.

"May I look up there?" she asked.

"I'll show you the way and turn on lights."

Upstairs, a single narrow hall ran through the house with doors on either side. It smelled a little close and musty up here, and Mrs. Bancroft opened a window at one end of the hall.

Susan studied the closed doors for a moment, trying to figure directions in her head. "Let's see —if the rooms on this side were at the back of the house, then there ought to be a tower on this corner. Would a bedroom there include the tower?"

"I'd like to look at this room, please."

The housekeeper pushed open the door. "There you are. I made it up fresh this afternoon, so if you like it, you can move right in."

Back home in the crowded apartment in New York, Susan's room had been a tiny makeshift, hardly more than a big closet. And the window had looked out upon a dreary gray air shaft. This might be a room with a view. Kindling in anticipation, Susan picked up her suitcase and went through the door.

The tower made a circular area in one corner, with a curving window seat all around. A bright rag rug, large and oval, lay in the middle of the floor, and the bed was a four-poster with a light patchwork quilt thrown across it. Against one wall stood a graceful old-fashioned chest of drawers, and near a window was a round pedestal table with an easy chair pulled up beside it.

"Tomorrow," Mrs. Bancroft said, "I'll bring you a proper dressing table from one of the other rooms. And you can have anything else that suits you. This was Gene's room, and he wanted everything real plain and shipshape."

Gene's room? Somehow that was disturbing. Susan would rather have had a room she wouldn't feel she was taking away from him. But the little room with the tower drew her, and she did not want to give it up.

"Bathroom's two doors down the hall," Mrs. Bancroft said. "You can have it all for your own now. Sure you won't be lonesome way up here by yourself?"

Susan had not thought of that, but she liked the room so much that she wouldn't think of it now.

"I'll be fine," she said. "And it won't seem lonesome when my family gets here."

After Mrs. Bancroft had gone, she closed the door and turned off the overhead lamp. With the room dark, she went to the tower alcove and knelt on the padded green cushions of the window seat. She pushed open a window and leaned her arms upon the sill, looking out upon the wide, dark vista of starry sky, breathing in the clean, brisk air. A wind was blowing up, sweeping the sky clear of clouds, sighing in the pines, bringing with it a touch of chill to the night air. Out there under the stars lay the Hudson, a curving band of dark velvet. Lights rimmed the highway on the opposite shore and reflected themselves on the surface of the river. Pairs of lights, like matched beads, marched across Bear Mountain Bridge, and the beacon high on Anthony's Nose flashed red, then white, evenly, again and again.

No, she wouldn't give up this room with its high, tremendous view. Not even if it had belonged to Gene and he might not like the thought of having her in it.

She turned on the lights again and opened the door to the hall. The corridor stretched dimly toward the stairs, and the house seemed very still. Aunt Edith's rooms were down a floor and on the other side.

The words Miss Altoona had spoken that morning returned unbidden to Susan's mind. What had she meant about Sarah Teague's threatening to come back and haunt this house? That was silly, of course. No one except Miss Altoona would believe in such things. Besides, Sarah Teague could have nothing against the Prices. They were really helping her family in its time of need.

The sound of a cuckoo clock calling the hour from the depths of the house broke the silence, and Susan closed her door quickly. The sound seem eerie at this distance. But here inside her room she was safe and snug. If anything haunted this room, it would be Gene's resentful thoughts, and those were something she might eventually deal with.

Putting aside her momentary uneasiness, she began to unpack her suitcase.

9

A Mark on the Floor

Aunt Edith came up to visit her before long, bringing a tray with a pitcher of hot chocolate on it and plump blue earthenware mugs. The chocolate bubbled into the cups as Aunt Edith poured, and a warm, luscious aroma rose with the steam.

With her mug in hand, Aunt Edith went over to admire the tower view. This was a lovely room, she said, and undoubtedly the house would seem less quiet when Adam arrived.

So Aunt Edith, too, had noticed the stillness. But she said nothing about its being lonely up here and seemed to understand exactly why Susan wanted this room.

"Don't sit up too late reading, Sue dear," she warned knowingly just as she left. "We'll need to be up early to make use of the morning. If you want me for anything, just pound on the radiator. But pound hard, so I'll hear you. I can sleep pretty soundly sometimes."

When her aunt had gone, Susan got ready for bed, reassured by the knowledge that she could bring someone upstairs quickly if she wanted to. After all, this had been Gene's room, and he had not minded being alone at the top of the house.

With her pajamas on, she took one more satisfying look out the window. Then she climbed into bed under the gay patchwork quilt and fluffed up the pillow behind her back. A low chest of drawers stood beside the bed, and upon it was a small lamp with a pewter candlestick for a base. Susan tilted the shade in order to get better light and reached for the book she had brought with her.

It was not a book from the library this time, but the book about old sailing ships from the Teague barrel. She was more interested than ever now to learn about the *Flying Sarah*, its captain, Rufus Teague, and his wife.

She turned to the picture of the *Sarah* and began to read the text on the page beside it. At first the author dealt only with a description of the ship, a discussion of its design, and of the builder who had created it. Susan skipped through most of this, hoping to find out more about the Teague family. Her reward was greater than she expected.

When he got around to it, the author delighted in telling the tragic tale of Captain Teague's last voyage. The Captain had been far from a young man at the time, though still vigorous and active. He had sailed the oceans of the world most of his life, and he knew the countries and peoples of the Far East very well. In China he had a good friend whom he was trying to serve on his last trip—a wealthy mandarin in Hong Kong. This man had commissioned his trusted friend Captain Teague to bring a valuable gift of jewels from India to please the mandarin's chief wife. Captain Rufus had those jewels aboard the *Flying Sarah* when he sailed into pirate waters in the China Sea for the last time. Always before, he had been skillful in evading the pirates that threatened the area around Hong Kong Island, but perhaps they had wind this time of the booty he carried. At any rate, they attacked more persistently than usual and managed to board his ship. The Captain himself stood by his men in the fighting, and he was killed along with others who fell mortally wounded. The pirates stripped the ship of everything of value, including the jewels in the Captain's trust. The *Sarah* had limped into Hong Kong, crippled and several days delayed. Captain Rufus had been buried with his men in the China Sea.

The story was doubly moving because it was about real people whose descendants Susan knew. And it did not stop with the Captain's death. Afterward his widow, Sarah Teague, had taken on the debt of the jewels that had been lost in her husband's care. He had been trusted with their delivery and she would not see that trust betrayed, even though what had happened was no fault of his. What tears she must have wept had been in private, for not even her children were allowed to see evidence of her sorrow and despair. She wore the black of mourning from that time on, but she carried herself with stern pride and took a new interest in her late husband's business, and in the ships he had owned and sailed—among them the ill-fated *Flying Sarah.*

But while she would often board other ships of the company, legend had it that never again did she set foot on the decks of the *Sarah.* Eventually, to help raise the money so badly needed, the ship was sold out of the family.

It was not until after Sarah Teague's death that the mandarin friend of her husband was finally repaid in full by the family for the gems that were never delivered. Though the Teagues were left vastly poorer for Sarah's action, they had approved and stood by her. The honor of Rufus Teague was something valued more than wealth.

The writer concluded:

Some time after his father was murdered by pirates, Teague's oldest son had a house built on the banks of the Hudson River, and this house remained in the family, despite its impoverished state. It was to her son's home that Sarah Teague came in her last years, and there are stories about her that persist to the present day. People say that she has left her own strong mark upon the house and that only Teagues can live in it comfortably.

Years after his mother was gone, the younger Captain Teague, who sailed a steamship across the Atlantic, took his family abroad for a trip, and rented the house in their absence. But the new people did not stay for long. They complained that no matter how carefully they locked the doors, trespassers found their way in—particularly a tall woman in black with a strong, sad face. They did not like the way she looked at them through the windows, or the outrageous way in which she walked about the hallways whenever she could get inside. The matter was never fully explained, and townspeople said that the intruder was Sarah Teague. Others, more sensible, suggested that the new family merely wanted to break its lease and chose this made-up story to manage it. In any event, the house was never again left in outside hands.

"(Until now," Susan thought uneasily.)

At this writing, the Teague house still stands upon the high banks of the Hudson, and its turrets may be seen by the voyager traveling upriver by boat.

Held in spite of a chilly feeling down her spine, Susan read to the last word. This must be the story that was the basis of Altoona Heath's words of warning. Susan wished now that she had read it in broad daylight when her aunt was nearby. To read it late at night in this tower room of the Teague house, with all the third floor dark and empty outside her door, did not make for easy slumber.

She turned the page idly and came upon an old photograph of Captain Rufus Teague and his wife, Sarah. The Captain, in full uniform, sat looking out at the camera rather fiercely. His muttonchop whiskers and walrus mustache hid most of his face from view, but he looked like a man who could easily rule the seas. Sarah seemed to be cut from the same solid granite that had patterned her husband. In the picture she stood beside him, one hand resting on his shoulder in the old-fashioned way. Her hair was drawn back from a severe forehead, and her eyes were set deep above a strong, full-fleshed nose. There was little nonsense, and nothing of humor, about her wide mouth. The look of it, as well as the set of her chin, reminded Susan a little of Sarah's great-great-great-grandson, Gene Foster.

Sarah Teague, Susan decided, was not the sort of person she would want to meet unexpectedly in a dim hallway at night, if the Captain's wife did not approve of her being there. She closed the book and laid it aside on the bed table.

When she settled down to sleep, she left the lamp burning. Outside, the wind sighed past her window and rustled the nearby branches of trees with unseen fingers. Susan thought of that strange weeping beech not far from the house, and wondered if a black-garbed figure with deep-set eyes might be lurking in its shadows, waiting for the house to sleep before stirring abroad.

Such a thought made her angry with herself. She turned over impatiently under the covers. "You're not really scared," she told herself. "And you don't believe in ghost stories. You're stirring all this up in your own mind and it's not necessary at all."

Once Adam had told her that she liked to scare herself, and she denied it now furiously. She did *not* like it and she would stop it at once. She closed her eyes and took long, deep breaths, counting each one up to twenty, then starting over. By the time she reached the third twenty she was asleep.

The hour of midnight came and the cuckoo clock called the hour in the silent house. Outside, a few clouds rode the sky, driven like sheep before the wind. At a moment when the moon's face was covered by white fleece, the branches of the weeping beech tree stirred and parted. A shadowy figure emerged from hiding and moved toward the house. As if its purpose was certain, it mounted the steps and went through the back door, which Mrs. Bancroft had locked securely before she went to bed. As if it knew these corridors well, the figure moved through the kitchen and the back hall toward the front of the house. There was something ungainly about its motion, as if, perhaps, it had not walked the living earth for some time.

Emerging in the great hall that was the baronial living room of the house, it went first to the foot of the stairway and stood there for a moment, as though for the first time undecided. The room was dark as a cave with the moon behind a cloud, but the visitor seemed to need no light. After a moment of quiet at the foot of the stairs, it moved again across the room to a place at the side of the great fireplace. Its hands sought the walls, searching, searching, touching lightly, moving on. A ray of moonlight escaped the cloud and glowed faintly at a window. In the pale light two pale hands moved above the shadowy figure as the search went on.

It was a jarring thump that shook the house that wakened Susan. She sat straight up in bed, as though a cord had jerked her upright, and listened with all her senses. The tower windows were silvered with moonlight, and the pewter lamp beside her bed shed a pool of warmer light nearby. The house was silent, yet she knew that all was not well.

Somewhere, far below, something had moved that should not move. Surely she had not dreamed that vibrating thump. With her heart beating in her throat, she ran to the door and pressed her ear against the panel, listening. The silence was no longer complete. There was a sound from the depths of the house—something muffled and strange that she could not identify.

It took all the courage she possessed to open the door and look out into the hall. Near the stairway hung a single cord with a shaded bulb burning at the end of it. Every door along the hallway was closed, and nothing stirred in the upper regions of the house. But now she could hear the muffled sound more clearly—as if something heavy was being dragged across a floor. She thought of pounding her shoe on the radiator to waken Aunt Edith, but that would give the signal all through the house that these strange goings on had been heard.

Barefooted, she stepped onto the cool, carpetless boards of the hall and tiptoed toward the stairs. The second step creaked beneath her feet, and the fifth and the eighth. Then she was on the floor below, hurrying now toward her aunt's door. She thrust it open and called softly through the darkness.

"Aunt Edith! Aunt Edith! Wake up! There's somebody moving around downstairs."

Her aunt sat up sleepily and turned on the bedside lamp. Once more the house was still.

"Perhaps you were dreaming, Sue dear," Aunt Edith said. "I don't hear a thing. Or perhaps Mrs. Bancroft got up for something. If you don't feel comfortable up there alone, bring your pillow and covers down and sleep on the couch in my room."

But Susan could not accept so easy a dismissal of what she had heard. The sounds had been real, not part of any dream.

"We could go out and look over the balcony rail," she whispered. "If we went quietly and turned on the light, we might catch whoever it was."

Aunt Edith yawned and stretched and got out of bed somewhat limply. Clearly she was doing this only to humor Susan and reassure her. Her quilted bedroom slippers made no more sound than Susan's bare feet as the two of them stole along the balcony toward the light switch. It was Susan's finger that found the switch and sent the room below leaping to reality in a great wave of illumination. The switch had turned on the overhead chandelier and several wall sconces as well. The daytime shadows were gone, and the room lay bright and revealed—and empty. For an instant something touched the skin of Susan's face lightly and was gone.

"Did you feel that?" she cried. "Did you feel that breath of wind?"

Aunt Edith nodded. "There must be a window open somewhere below. Let's go down and see. Perhaps the sounds you heard were outside."

They descended to the empty, undisturbed room, and Susan ran to the front door. It was securely locked. But beside it a window that looked out upon the veranda stood half open, and the night wind fluttered its lacy curtains. Aunt Edith shook her head over this neglect on Mrs. Bancroft's part and closed the window, fastening the latch. Then she walked to the rear of the house and tried the securely locked back door. As she followed her aunt about, Susan could hear Mrs. Bancroft's even snoring from her bedroom at the rear of the house. Apparently an army could come in and the housekeeper would never stir.

Aunt Edith yawned again. "You see, dear? It was just the breeze blowing through that open window. Probably you heard the draperies thudding against the wall."

Susan shook her head. She could not accept so easy an explanation. As Aunt Edith started upstairs, Susan paused in the living room, looking intently about the brightly lighted area. The summer hearth was cold and unused, the fire screen in place. The marble mantel gleamed fresh and clean, and the polished wood of the wall panels on either side was visible, their surfaces plain, revealing nothing, the two mirrors against them reflecting the room. But there was something wrong. She knew it with all her being, and yet it was nothing she could explain.

A sudden impulse to escape this room and its mystery seized her and she turned to run toward the stairs. One bare foot stepped insecurely upon a small rug, and the rug went flying, spilling Susan to the floor.

"Oh dear!" Aunt Edith said. "That was a nasty fall. Have you hurt yourself, dear?"

The floor was hard and she had come down hard. The fall had hurt, but four brothers had taught her to keep from showing pain, however jarring. In any case, her interest was caught by something else. The rug, in sliding, had left something clearly revealed on the polished floor of the room. There beside Susan was a long, deep scratch across the dark wood.

She reached out gingerly and touched the scar with her finger. This was no old mark, polished over many times. The wood showed white the whole length of the scratch, and there were tiny splinters of wood in the jagged places. It was quite clear that something had been recently dragged across this very floor.

10

The Face in the Pool

Susan returned to her own bed after all, even though Aunt Edith's invitation to finish the night on the couch in her room had been tempting. Later, she knew, she would want to tell Adam about what had happened tonight, and she would not want to confess that she had been too frightened to go back to bed in her own room.

So here she was, not counting sheep or her own breathing, but counting noses, as it were.

Aunt Edith's explanation of the scratch had been simple enough: "Probably Captain Dan made it this afternoon when he was moving his things. A trunk being pulled across the floor could have left a mark."

Susan suspected that Captain Dan would have taken great care *not* to make such a scratch with a trunk or anything else, but she did not say so. Aunt Edith still thought she had been dreaming, and it seemed no use to try to describe sounds to her aunt that were so hard to identify.

So now she was going over the possibilities in her own mind. Somehow she didn't believe the intruder was an ordinary burglar. Nothing seemed to have been taken or disturbed in the room. That left three people who might fit into the mystery. First, there was the Captain, though Susan was not inclined to suspect him. What Captain Dan wanted from the house, he would come and take openly. Next came Gene. Although Gene had come into the shop to look at those books and had meant to take one away, it seemed unlikely that he would do a thing like this. What could he possibly want to sneak out of the house and conceal in the dead of night? If the house had a secret, why not let it alone, since the Captain had not yet decided to sell?

The third person was Altoona Heath. Miss Altoona was certainly capable of being elaborately foolish, and she admitted to a strong interest in the Teague secret. But for a grown person to be guilty of burglary just to satisfy a whim seemed hard to believe. It was hard, as well, to imagine the large Altoona climbing in and out of windows.

That was the trouble with this whole thing. No one Susan could think of really fitted the "crime"— if there was a crime. At least no one who was now living.

She closed her eyes and began to breathe deeply and quickly, counting as fast as she could. Because there was one solution that she did not mean to harbor for even a moment. If Sarah Teague walked these corridors, she certainly wasn't made of the stuff that would leave long, clear scratches on a floor.

Surprisingly, the breathing trick worked once more, for she fell asleep in the middle of it, and did not waken again until the early morning sun shone against her tower windows. When she opened her eyes and saw the sun, she rolled out of bed and went straightway to see her view by daylight.

Above the hills on the far side of the Hudson the sun was coming up in a sky of pink and aquamarine, embroidered with threads of gray cloud. It touched the world with a rosy glow and gave the river a shading of pale pink. From the water the hill climbed steeply on this side, the trees hiding Gene's big rock down in the clearing. Thick woods marched right to the edge of the level place where the Teague house stood, with only the strange beech tree encroaching on Teague ground.

Susan moved around the window seat to another window of the tower and looked out the side toward the glade in the woods where the quiet pool lay hidden. She could just glimpse the gleam of its water among the trees. "How had Sarah Teague come to meet her death in such a place?" she wondered.

However, there was too much to do this morning to dwell long on such thoughts. She wanted to unpack and fix up her room in as pleasant a fashion as possible. With her own possessions spread about, as there had been no space to spread them at Aunt Edith's, she could make the room look more like hers and less like Gene's. It still left her faintly uncomfortable to think that she was taking the room away from Gene.

Once or twice that morning she went downstairs to look about the living room, searching for anything that might be different, that might give her a clue as to what had happened in the night. Mrs.

Bancroft had discovered the scratch and gone to work on it with floor wax. It still looked like a fresh scar, and Mrs. Bancroft hid it from view with the rug.

Susan's most interesting discovery of the morning came shortly before lunch, when she was in her room cutting shelf paper to fit into the drawers of a tall chest which Aunt Edith had admired.

"It's a fine old New England piece," her aunt had told her. "Walnut—quite plain, but beautiful in line and proportion. You can see that the bottom part is slightly larger than the upper chest that is set upon it. That lower part, like a dressing table, is called a lowboy. When a chest of drawers is set on top of it, it becomes a highboy."

Susan was more interested in the use to which she could put the chest, however. The lowboy part had a small, deep drawer on either side, with a shallower drawer in the middle. She decided to fit the three with paper before she went to work on the long drawers of the upper chest. Small brass handles served to pull out the drawers, and she found that the middle drawer stuck rather badly. When she got it open, she pulled it all the way out to see what had caused it to jam.

Reaching into the opening, she found that something knobby had caught in the space at the back of the drawer. The thing felt odd and lumpy in her fingers, and when she pulled it out, she found it was a string of wooden beads. The individual beads were large as a cherry in size, and the strand was not very long. When she held it about her throat, she found the strand was of choker length.

The beads were made of a beautiful dark-red wood that seemed different from mahogany. Probably someone had carved each sphere by hand. On alternate beads a tiny flower and miniature design had been cut into the wood.

She took her find down to Aunt Edith, who was working in her own rooms. Her aunt examined the beads with interest. This was something that must be shown to Captain Teague, she said. He would undoubtedly know its history and to whom it had belonged. Clearly, it was rather old. The uneven planes on the round beads were not at all like a machine-made product.

After lunch Susan wandered outside to look at the little pool that had such a dark history behind it. The glade was as quiet as she remembered it. She sat down on the log that protruded into the water and watched the dappling movement of sun and leaf shadows on the pale-green surface. The aura of green came mainly from the reflection of trees and shrubbery and did not reach into the center.

A splash from a rock near the bank made her turn in time to see a turtle flop into the water. There must be all sorts of curious living creatures down there in the pool's depths. Yet it was such a small pool—not at all like the big lake up near the highway. How had it been possible for a grown person to drown in such a place? Surely it couldn't be very deep, even out in the middle.

She stood up and inched her way along the log toward the spot where it vanished under water. Below skittering water bugs on the surface, the depths of the pool were somberly lighted by the sun. Susan could see thick, oozy mud on the shallow bottom and small, darting fish playing around an old tree stump submerged beneath the water. When a breeze ruffled the surface, it wrinkled like silk, then smoothed into glassy stillness, very clear and transparent.

As she stared at it, what she had thought was a brown tree stump took on a strange shape—a shape that was almost human. A face seemed to be looking up at her from the bottom of the pool. The nose and mouth were clearly marked, as were the hollow eyes that watched her with hypnotic intensity. Knowing perfectly well that it could not be a real face she saw, Susan had the feeling, nevertheless, that the haunting eyes commanded her, that they asked something of her that she must not refuse.

She wrenched her gaze from the water, compelling herself to look at the treetops, green and feathery against the yellow-bright sky of early afternoon. The face was an optical illusion, of course. It wasn't really there. Old chunks of wood often seemed to have pictures in them. Or it might be just an oddly worn rock.

When she had blinked a few times to clear her vision, she looked into the water again. The face was still there, staring straight up at her. It looked much more like a real face than any stump or rock she had ever seen. She edged back to shore and searched the bushes nearby for a long stick. Then she returned to her position on the log. Carefully she reached down through the water to prod the chunk of log or rock, or whatever it was that looked like a face. But the stick slipped off onto the bottom, and mud surged up like dull brown smoke through the water, clouding everything.

The face was lost in the murk, and Susan knew it would take some time for the mud she had churned up to settle so that she could look down through clear water again. Somehow she did not want to wait. The loneliness of the place made her uneasy, as it had before. She thought of Sarah Teague who had died here so strangely, so tragically, and who, legend had it, still haunted this vicinity. Panic seized her. She was suddenly more frightened than she had been last night over the queer sounds in the house.

Almost running, she took the road that led past Altoona Heath's house and around the end of the big lake. The everyday sound of cars swishing past on the highway was reassuring. When she reached it, she found herself opposite the firehouse, with the red pyramid structure on its tower that she knew now was a fire siren.

The door to the engine station stood open, and Susan could see Gene Foster working with one of the men, polishing the metal trim on an engine. Apparently he was taking his new membership in the company seriously.

Waiting her chance, Susan crossed the highway when traffic cleared and approached the open door. Gene looked up and saw her.

"Hi," he said. "The women are upstairs, if you're looking for them. They're getting things ready for the firemen's fair. It's coming up this week, you know."

At the moment, Susan was not especially interested in the fair. She wanted to get Gene to talk.

"Do they have many fires in Highland Crossing?" she asked.

The fireman smiled at her and went toward the back of the engine room, leaving Gene to answer her question.

"Not many. It's *people* who cause most fires, and Grandfather sees to it that there is a lot of fire prevention education, so everyone around here is careful. Most fires needn't happen. Or else they could be easily put out when they start, if people knew what to do and didn't lose their heads."

He stopped polishing and regarded her critically. "For instance, what would you do if you were in your living room and there was a short in some wire that started a fire?"

Susan suspected that she would scream loudly and get out of the room as fast as possible, but she felt that Gene would not approve of such hysterical action, so she tried to offer something more constructive.

"I'd get a pan of water from the kitchen and throw it on the fire," she said, feeling rather pleased with the picture of herself being coolheaded in the face of danger.

Gene snorted scornfully. "That would be the worst thing you could do! You'd probably get yourself electrocuted and spread the fire besides. Water conducts electricity, and you *never* throw water on an electric fire. The first thing to do would be to pull out the plug if it was in a place where you could reach it easily. Then you might use a thick chair cushion or a blanket to smother the fire—if you could get at it. Of course, you should be yelling for help at the same time. A fire is something for grown-ups to handle. Most fires start small, and they can be smothered with thick cloth, or sand, or put out with water from a hose, if they're not electric."

Susan leaned against one of the big swinging doors of the firehouse, listening with interest.

"I know you don't put water on a grease fire," she said, wanting to show some knowledge of these matters. "Water only spatters a grease fire and throws it around. We had one in a frying pan at home once, and Mom smothered it with the cover to the pan. It went right out, but it scared us all for a minute."

"If people would think about what to do ahead of time, they wouldn't get so scared," Gene said, sounding a little like his grandfather. "Of course, if a real fire gets going, then you don't stick around. You get out as fast as you can, and never mind what you want to save. It's not the fire that's so dangerous—it's the smoke. Even firemen have to watch that, because it can get a man before he knows what's happening."

Gene reached up alongside one of the engines and brought down a box. There was a smoke mask inside, and he took it out and put it on, looking at Susan through the goggles like a man from outer space. She had to laugh, but Gene did not regard the matter as funny. He removed the mask and put it back in its box.

"When firemen go into a burning building, they always go in two at a time, so one won't be left in danger alone," he explained. "And the first two who go in to locate the fire source wear masks. But of course you wouldn't have a mask at home. So if you smell smoke in the night and get up, you take precautions. Like feeling the bedroom door, or the cellar door, or whatever, before you open it. If it feels hot, you don't open it at all. You start looking for some other way out. Maybe if you're upstairs you go to the windows and yell for help. But don't lose your head and jump out. With doors closed, there'll probably be plenty of time for somebody to get to you."

"What if the door isn't closed to start with?" Susan asked.

Gene was clearly enjoying his role of informant, and he went on readily. "If there's smoke and you have to get out through it, then the safest place is down on the floor. Warm air rises, and the smoke with it, so the air near the floor will be best to breathe. It's a good idea to put a bathrobe over your head, or if you're near water, soak a towel and wrap it around your face and head. Of course, if your clothes catch fire, *don't run*—roll! Lots of people have died because they went dashing around like a flaming torch."

Susan shivered. She did not, she felt, want to know anything more about fires. "You're scaring me. Let's talk about something else."

Again Gene made a snorting sound of scorn, sounding just like Adam when he was disgusted with her. "Don't act like an ostrich! If you think about these things ahead of time, you'll be in much less danger than if you don't. Grandfather tells people to have fire drills right in their own homes. Every member of the family ought to know just what he would do under any circumstances that might come up. Most people don't even know how to go to the phone and put through a fire call. And when they do get the firehouse, they start yelling so they can't be understood. Or they forget to give the address and hang up too soon. The fireman who answers the phone here has to be good at calming excited people and getting all the information he needs."

"I suppose you're right," Susan admitted reluctantly.

Gene reached up on one of the trucks and took down a big green horn with a handle that made it look like a spaceman's gun, complete with trigger, and said: "Get out of the way! Here they come!"

The words blared out of the horn well magnified, and Susan nearly jumped out of her shoes. She looked around in terror and saw that nothing at all was coming. Gene was practically bent over, laughing at the way he'd startled her.

"This is a bull horn," he said. "The chief uses it to give orders at a fire."

"A typical boy's trick," Susan thought in annoyance. She felt much less like saving Gene's feelings now. Indeed, she would like to pay him back for the scare.

"Mrs. Bancroft said the tower room I picked was your room," she said tartly. She might as well let him know that she knew, and didn't care! "This morning I found something jammed behind one of the drawers in the highboy. It was a string of wooden beads. Do you know whose they are?"

Gene looked interested. "Carved wooden beads? They're mine. I lost them ages ago and never could find them. I'll be glad to have them back."

A string of beads seemed an odd thing for a boy to value, but she wouldn't keep them if he wanted them.

"I'll give them to you next time you come to the house," Susan said. Let him come after them if he wanted them. She decided to try him next with the face in the pool. "I saw something strange down in the woods just now. You know that little pool near your house? I was standing on a log down there a little while ago and I saw a face in the water staring up at me. It was a queer, brown face with deep, staring eyes—awfully spooky."

Gene was returning the bull horn to its place on the truck, and for a moment he had his back to her. He did not look around, and her information did not seem to interest him.

"Probably it was an old rock," he said. "Or maybe just your own reflection."

"I know what I look like," Susan said. Nothing seemed to surprise this boy, but she knew how she could really startle him. "Last night," she announced abruptly, "somebody broke into your house."

This time his reaction was more satisfactory. He had just picked up his polishing cloth, and he stared at her with it hanging limply from his fingers.

"What do you mean—broke in?" he demanded.

"I heard someone," Susan said. "So I got Aunt Edith and we went downstairs and found a window open. But there was nobody there. Whoever it was must have heard us and got away."

"Maybe you were just dreaming," Gene said, and began to polish again.

Susan shook her head. "There was someone there all right. I found a long scratch on the floor that had been covered by a rug. A new scratch."

Gene opened his mouth, but whatever he meant to say did not come. The direction of his gaze shifted to something behind Susan. She looked around quickly and saw that Altoona Heath was standing above them on the steps to what had once been the schoolhouse. She carried a large shopping bag, and she was looking at them with a lively interest, as if she might have been listening for some time. When she saw they had noticed her, she urged Susan on.

"Did someone really break into the Teague house last night? What happened? Did you call the police?"

"We—we aren't sure anybody really broke in," Susan admitted reluctantly. "Aunt Edith found a window open, and she said I might have heard noises from outside."

"But you said there was a scratch on the floor?" Altoona was persistent.

Susan nodded. "Yes—as though something heavy had been dragged across the living room."

"How very strange!" Miss Altoona said. "Now what was that about a face you saw in the little pool?"

Gene said, "I've got work to do," and went toward the back of the firehouse. He had clearly had enough of Miss Altoona.

"I don't suppose the face was really anything," Susan said. "I'm always seeing faces in logs and rocks and things." Somehow she didn't want to admit how frightened she had been.

"Now that's very interesting," Miss Altoona said. "I do exactly the same sort of thing. When I was a child, my sister used to get very impatient with me. She said I had too much imagination."

Susan found it hard to believe that Miss Altoona had ever been a child. That was too great a feat for her own imagination.

The woman shifted the weight of her bag in her arms. "I'd better take these things for the fair inside. By the way, I've been reading some of those books you suggested. They're really good stories—I'm enjoying them."

She went up the steps, and Susan was left alone in front of the firehouse. Alone with her own puzzling thoughts. Without planning it that way, she had confronted two of her "suspects" with her knowledge of what had happened last night. And neither one had given any indication of guilt. Of course, either one could be covering up and hiding any possible alarm in order to fool her.

At any rate, she was now left with only one more person—Captain Dan. Or perhaps two, if she were willing to count a woman named Sarah Teague. Not, she reminded herself hastily, that she would want to confront *her!*

II

Adam

Nᴏᴛʜɪɴɢ ᴡᴀs seen of Captain Dan during the rest of that day. Nor did Gene come to the house for the string of hand-carved beads. When he did come, Susan meant to show him the clipper-ship book at the same time. Since that book had been stored with other old books for so many years in the Teague attic, it might be that neither he nor his grandfather knew it existed.

For the rest of the day Susan helped her aunt in one way or another. There were still things to be brought up from the shop and a room to be prepared for Adam's arrival tomorrow. Aunt Edith suggested that Susan choose a room for Adam, so that they could have it ready to welcome him. If he decided to pick a different one later, that would be all right.

Choosing a room for her brother took a good deal of consideration. She decided finally on a room on the third floor toward the front of the house, where there was a small, screened-in porch. Adam could use the porch as a place to keep all the stuff he never wanted to put away, but which Mother didn't like to see cluttering his bedroom. The extra space might coax Adam to stay up here on the third floor where he would keep his sister company.

The choice involved making some shifts in furniture in order to pick things Adam would be most likely to find useful. Also, as Susan warned Aunt Edith, it might be just as well not to give him the best antiques in the house, because he was always rather hard on furniture. Besides, he wouldn't pay much attention to the appearance of things. Adam's mind was usually on other matters.

"Such as?" Aunt Edith asked.

"Oh, sports and games. And making things. Adam is wonderful with tools. He'll be good at repairing whatever goes wrong around the house. Much better than Dad."

Susan was glad to be really tired when she went to bed that night. There was only one more night to get through before she would have company on this floor. And surely she could manage until then. If she was awfully sleepy, she would not lie awake and listen for phantom footsteps or for thudding sounds downstairs in the living room.

Unfortunately, being so sleepy that she fell sound asleep almost as soon as her head touched the pillow did not guarantee that she would stay asleep all through the night. Just as she had awakened around midnight the night before, she came wide-awake again tonight. Perhaps it was that saucy bird in the cuckoo clock that roused her with its prolonged announcements at midnight. Whatever it might be, here she was, awake and listening once more to the sounds of the night.

Except for the occasional creaking of aging timbers, the house seemed still enough. Outside, insects hummed a loud chorus, and the frogs in the little pool were croaking like anything. This time it was the sudden silence of the frogs that startled her. Without warning, every frog sound stopped, and she could imagine one big bullfrog giving a signal, so that they all sat around on logs and rocks, bulgy-eyed with staring, the sacs at their throats heaving in and out as they listened.

The desire to look out the tower windows was irresistible to Susan. It was warmer than last night, and the night air was light and gentle against her face as she knelt on the seat cushions and looked out toward the pool where the frog orchestra was having an intermission.

The sharp crackle of a twig reached her—broken perhaps beneath a foot—and she drew in her breath sharply. Then she saw the lights. There seemed to be two separate points of light down there near the pool. Two lanterns were moving about.

Something was certainly going on down there. Even as she watched, the lights disappeared completely, and after a brief interval, the frogs started in again, announcing that all was clear. The sense of something happening out there in the night had vanished, and Susan gave up and returned to bed. There was no use in disturbing Aunt Edith again, when she would have nothing to show her. The shaded lanterns had never revealed the persons who carried them. And besides, people who went about openly with lanterns in hand could not be engaged in anything very wrong.

More than ever, she wished Adam were already here. If there was something queer going on, then he would be the best person possible to have on her side in working out the mystery. His mind moved in straight lines. It wasn't like hers—darting off down every entrancing side trail, with a resulting confusion of thought she did not know how to cure. Of course, the difficult thing would be to convince Adam that there really was a mystery and that she hadn't imagined the whole thing. Once he believed, he would help her, and they would get speedily to the root of whatever was going on.

Tuesday morning finally arrived. The house was stocked with extra groceries against the arrival of a boy with a large appetite. When Aunt Edith opened the shop, Susan went with her. The bus stop was so close to the Old Oak that she could sit on the steps and see the bus coming.

She was ready long before it was due, and fortunately it was on time. She glimpsed it the moment it came around the curve of the highway, and she called out to let Aunt Edith know. Then she tore down the path along the edge of the road, to arrive at the stop just as the air brakes brought the bus to a gliding halt.

Adam swung down the steps, suitcase in hand, looking big and brown and healthy. Because she was getting used to Gene, who was thin and rather slight after his long months in a hospital, Susan found her brother even larger than she had remembered. She would have liked to hug him, but she knew he didn't approve of "sloppiness," so she stood there with her hands in the pockets of her jeans and said, "Hello," her face alight with smiles. She was pleased and surprised when he was the one to hug her.

Adam's reddish hair was rumpled as usual, and he had managed to get a streak of grease across his white shirt. Mom said he had a magnetic effect upon grease. If there was any within a mile, it immediately attached itself to Adam. His grin was at its wide and cheerful best, and even more freckles than she remembered had popped out across his nose.

"Hi, kid," he said, looking really pleased to see her. "Boy, am I glad to get out of New York! What a boring town in the summertime!"

The word "boring" was not in Susan's vocabulary. How was it possible to be bored in a world where there were always more fascinating things to do and learn than any one person could manage in a lifetime? However, she knew what her brother meant. It was harder to do the physical, outdoor things Adam liked best in New York. They were there, but you had to hunt for them.

Together they walked back to the shop, where Aunt Edith stood on the steps, waiting to greet her nephew.

The three of them had lunch in the room back of the shop that day, and then Aunt Edith closed up long enough to drive Adam and his suitcase down to the Teague house. There she left him in Susan's hands and hurried back to work.

Adam's reaction to the old house was one of greater interest than Susan would have expected. She discovered the reason rather quickly.

"That railing needs mending," he pointed out as they climbed to the front door. "I wonder if there are any tools around the place."

"Captain Dan has a toolroom downstairs, and he hasn't moved everything out. He'll probably let you use whatever you want. He said there were more things to be done around a house than he could get to any more, so he'll probably be glad of your help. Come on upstairs and I'll show you your room. I picked it out for you myself."

To her relief, Adam was pleased with her choice. He saw the porch at once and approved it for the very reason Susan had in mind. Everything was turning out even better than she had hoped.

He didn't mind having Susan help with his unpacking, and she was glad for the chance to ask questions about home and the family. When he was through and had changed to jeans and a sport shirt, Susan offered to show him around outside. This suited Adam, but when she took him out to the rear of the house, he promptly started off in a direction of his own. He noticed the pool in the woods and headed for it, with Susan trailing after him on the run. In a way, it was nice to have Adam in charge again. There was always a good deal of action and excitement when he was around, and life was full of quick decisions. Sometimes too quick, as Dad often reminded him.

When he reached the edge of the pool, Adam studied the water with a practical eye. "Too shallow and too muddy for swimming," he said. "But there ought to be good bait for fishing in the earth around here. And I suppose there are lots of places to fish."

"I know a boy who can show you," Susan told him eagerly. "And there's a swimming pool in Bear Mountain Park." Then she plunged into the subject she had longed to talk to him about. "Adam, I'm glad you've come! Something awfully queer is going on around this place."

"What do you mean—queer?" Adam asked.

She had waited so long to tell him, that now it all rushed out end-to-end in a clutter of words. At first Adam seemed to pay little attention. He had found what looked like a hornets' nest up in a tree and was studying it with absorbed interest. She hoped he wouldn't decide to poke it, to see what would happen. When she came to the part of her story that concerned the noise in the night and the scratch on the floor, however, he forgot the hornets and stared at her, his attention arrested. She knew he had taken to reading detective stories lately, and watching mystery plays on television. The idea of a mystery in real life seemed to appeal to him. But he didn't mean to accept her views on the matter without challenge.

"Suppose Aunt Edith was right about your hearing noises from outside?" he said, tugging at a springy lock of red hair over his forehead.

Susan shook her head. "The noise was inside the house. It practically shook the whole place. That's what woke me up."

"A window opening, maybe?"

"No, I'm sure it wasn't that. It was more like something heavy falling to the floor with a jarring thud."

"Let's have a look when we get back to the house," Adam said, and walked out on the log that protruded into the pond.

Susan ran to the edge of the bank and called to him. "Don't stir up the water, but look down through it near the end of that log and tell me what you see."

He squatted on the log with the balance of a good athlete and peered into the water. "There are some bugs skittering around, and I think that's a turtle swimming out there. What am I supposed to see?"

"Is there a log or a rock or something on the bottom of the pool? Can you see it from where you are?"

He studied the water a while longer, then shook his head. "I can see a lot of weeds growing on the bottom here—it's fairly shallow."

She followed him out on the log and rested a hand on his shoulder to balance herself. But when she peered down through the quiet water, clearer now than it had been the other day, she could see nothing at all that resembled a face.

Adam listened while she told him what she had seen, and about lanterns moving among the trees down here. This time he was less impressed with her story, though he let her down gently without making fun of what she had said.

"Probably it was just the way the sunlight fell that made you think you saw a face in the water. And I suppose that anyone who wanted to walk through the woods at night would have to carry a lantern or a flashlight. It looks as though this path goes somewhere. Let's have a look."

She knew very well where it went. This was the path that dipped steeply down the hill toward Gene Foster's private basketball ground below. And she didn't want Adam to go down there until she'd had time to tell him about Gene.

But already it was too late. Having seen the path, Adam was all for action. He plunged down ahead of her, and there was nothing to do but follow breathlessly. She would catch up with him at the bottom, she thought, and get him to stop long enough to listen to what she had to tell him. Adam mustn't come upon Gene unprepared.

Adam reached the level opening before the

great rock wall ahead of her. Susan could see him below her through the trees. He didn't seem to notice the barrel hoop nailed to a tree, but he did see the rock.

When Susan reached the edge of the clearing, her brother had already started up the slanting rock side. He pulled himself up with greater ease and skill than Susan had managed, and she could only watch him in admiration. Fortunately, Gene was nowhere in sight. There was no stopping Adam, she knew, and she stood where she was to watch, leaning against the trunk of a tree where the woods ended at the clearing.

Adam was halfway up and enjoying himself, when around the lower buttress of rock, from the direction of the cabin below, came Gene Foster.

Susan started to call to him, and then checked her words. Perhaps Gene would go by without looking up at the rock. She had so wanted to have these two become friends, and with Gene so touchy about that rock he could no longer climb, everything would be spoiled if he saw Adam up there above his head.

Gene moved at his usual limping pace, and he did not glance toward the woods to see Susan standing there. But he heard Adam on the rock at once, and moved around to where he could look up at him. Susan saw the familiar dark scowl appear on his forehead, and knew that the worst possible thing was about to happen. There was no way to stop it. She could only stand there watching.

"Hey, you!" Gene called to Adam. "Don't you

know this is private property? You're trespassing!"

Adam poised himself upon a ledge three quarters of the way up and looked down at the boy on the ground below.

"I didn't see any sign," he said. "And I'm not hurting this hunk of rock."

Gene's face darkened. "That doesn't matter. Get down off there. You don't belong on this property."

The words did not ruffle Adam in the least. Susan knew he had sized up the slight, angry boy on the ground, and that he did not consider him much of an opponent.

"Come up and stop me if you want to," he said, and laughed out loud.

Gene must have realized that further words would be useless. Susan saw him brace himself, as if to get the best possible balance on his injured leg. But he made no other move for the moment. Adam reached the top and began to walk about the flat plateau above. The view of the Hudson and its hilly banks held him for only a moment before he moved on again. Susan hoped that he would miss the rock upon which letters and words had been chiseled, but he did not. She saw him stop and bend to read them. Then he came to the edge and looked down at Gene.

"Are you 'G. F.'?" he asked.

Gene stared at him without speaking, his resentment clearly rising.

"Isn't that sort of silly—claiming a rock?" Adam went on in a reasonable tone. "Like an explorer claiming the moon!"

This was more than Gene could take. "Come down here and I'll show you!" he shouted.

"O.K.," Adam said, more amused than angry.

He came down faster than he had gone up, jumping the last few feet to the ground, to land not far from Gene. But he made no move toward the slighter boy, merely standing poised and ready. Adam was no bully, as Susan knew, and he wouldn't fight a boy who was clearly weaker and smaller. But if Gene did anything crazy and reckless, Adam could easily knock him right across the clearing. And Gene would be helpless because of the crippled leg Adam had no knowledge of. Gene's rage was clearly smoldering, ready to explode. In a moment he would invite disaster.

Susan did the only thing she could think of. She hurled herself across the clearing between the two boys.

"That's my brother Adam!" she cried to Gene. "Don't you hit him! I won't let you hit him!"

Both boys stared in astonishment at this sudden stormy attack. Susan whirled away from Gene and faced her brother. She had to make this good, she had to make it convincing.

"Don't try to fight Gene Foster," she pleaded with Adam. "He knows how to box. He's awfully good at it. He'd beat you to pieces."

Neither boy made a move for a moment. Both looked in bewilderment at Susan and then at each other. It was Adam who began to laugh, and then, to her surprise, Gene seemed to come to his senses and see the joke as well. He laughed out loud, the sound as ringing and clear as Adam's own laughter. Susan was not sure she understood the joke, but it was such a relief to have them laughing together that she joined in.

In a moment everything might have been all right. But Gene, weak with laughter over the idea that *he* could really beat up a boy as big and healthy as Adam, took a step backward and lost his balance. He sat down hard upon the ground, and one leg of his jeans wrinkled upward, exposing the brace. Adam saw it, and spoke without thinking.

"Hey," he began, "I wouldn't fight a guy with only—" Then what he had been about to say came home to him, and he stopped in dismay.

But the damage had been done. Susan saw the flame of angry color sweep up Gene's face, clear to the edge of his thick, brown hair. She saw the rage in his gray eyes. He began to struggle to get up from the ground, and when Adam reached out to help him, he slapped the friendly hand away.

This was too much for Adam. "Let's get out of here," he said to Susan. "Your friend's a little crazy."

There was nothing to do but follow Adam up the path. She dared not stay to watch that humiliating struggle of Gene's to regain his feet. When he was up again, he would turn his anger on her if she was there.

As Adam climbed ahead, he threw questions back at her. "What's the matter with that fellow, anyway? What did he think he could do to me when he can't even stand up like other people?"

None of this had really been Adam's fault. He

had only been clumsy, not mean, Susan admitted to herself. But she couldn't bear to hear him criticize Gene.

"How would you feel," she demanded, "if an accident finished you for good in all the things you like to do best? Can't you imagine what it would be like to be Gene?"

Adam turned and looked down at her in surprise. He was not used to being talked back to by an adoring sister.

"How was I to know? Besides, if something like that happened to me, I'd have sense enough to see that I couldn't go around making people sore and trying to get into fights."

"Would you?" Susan asked stiffly.

Suddenly she didn't want the company of either Adam or Gene for one minute longer. She wanted to get off by herself where she could sit down and be quiet and think things out. Think how to mend what had been broken down there in the clearing.

She turned away from her brother and started off through the woods where there was no path and the hillside was steep and slippery with pine needles and dry leaves.

12

String of Beads

W HEN THE HILLSIDE finally opened upon the road that led to the highway, Susan followed it in the direction of the Old Oak. As she walked, a cloud she had not noticed until now blocked out the sun and there was a warning sprinkle of moisture. By the time she reached the antique shop, it had really begun to rain. But she didn't want to go inside where Aunt Edith might ask questions.

At the side of the shop, there among the marble figures, the summerhouse offered shelter. It was an old-fashioned gazebo, Aunt Edith had said, and for the moment it would do quite well as a retreat.

The little house was octagonal in shape, and its pointed roof slanted down in a deep overhang that sheltered the interior from rain. Susan went in and sat down on one of the benches, only to find that Boneless was there ahead of her. He uncoiled himself limply and came over to drape his length across her lap. She stroked him, finding his presence soothing as she listened to the unexpected downpour beating a tattoo on the roof. The afternoon had turned suddenly dark, and all about on the lawn the marble figures stood cool and white, with rain running off them in rivulets. The streaming curtain seemed to shut her away from the world, shut her in with her own long thoughts.

Most of all she wanted to think about exactly how she would feel if she were Gene. In all fairness, she wanted to understand how Adam felt too, though that was simpler. In neither case could she be sure of her conclusions because she was someone else, and she did not believe she would behave as either boy had behaved, even if she were in his shoes. The only thing she could be sure of was that more unpleasantness would not help matters. This was the time for a gesture of friendship, even if it wasn't immediately appreciated. Perhaps she had a good excuse for looking Gene up.

Almost as quickly as the shower had begun it ended, and the sun came out to set the world asparkle with raindrops. Water still dripped from the griffin's wings and from the marble fingers of the lady with the lyre. Susan set Boneless on the floor and hurried downhill toward the Teague house.

Adam was nowhere in sight, and she was glad not to meet him in the hallway as she went upstairs to her room. There she opened a drawer in the highboy and took out the string of wooden beads. For a moment, she hesitated over the book about clipper ships, then decided she would leave that for another time.

With the string of beads in her pocket, she went down through the dripping woods toward the cabin.

On the porch where Gene hung his punching bag,

Captain Dan sat in a rocker. He watched Susan skip across the stream and come up to the front of the cabin.

"Good afternoon," he said. "I was wishing for company."

But Susan had not come here to see the Captain. "Is Gene around?" she asked.

"He's around—somewhere," the captain said doubtfully. "But he's a bit on the mopey side today. Have you any notion about what's wrong?"

Susan sat down on the porch step and told him exactly what had happened between Gene and Adam. Captain Dan heard her out in silence, nodding now and then.

"Maybe it's a good thing, in the long run," he said when she was through. "Gene's afraid of being with other kids. He's afraid of going back to school. I guess he's ready to fight every inch of the way when he does. And all for fear he'll be pitied, or not accepted as an equal by the other boys."

"But why?" Susan pondered. "Why must he feel that way when it would be easier to let people be friendly and kind to him?"

Captain Dan sighed. "Sometimes people are too kind, and sometimes they aren't kind at all. We have to accept that. Physically, he won't be the other boys' equal, and that's what he can't face. One of the toughest things for most any human being to learn is how to live inside his own skin and like it. Some of the time we all want to be what we aren't. I guess part of growing up is finding out who we are and then going all out to do the best we can with what we have. Gene isn't ready yet to accept himself as he is and make something out of the very good things he's got."

As Susan thought about that, she absently took the string of beads from her pocket and began running them through her hands. The Captain stared at her.

"What's that you have there?" he asked.

Susan held up the beads. "I brought them down for Gene. They were stuck in a drawer in his room, and he said they were his."

The captain held out his hand, and she put the strand into it. His expression softened as he looked at the beads.

"They're very old," he said. "They were carved by my great-grandfather—by Captain Rufus Teague himself. Out of cherry wood that he got in Japan."

So that was why Gene valued them, Susan thought. But now he wasn't around so she could return them to him.

"Will you tell him I brought them down?" she said.

The Captain nodded, still dreaming over the beads. "I've heard stories about how Rufus Teague was quite an artist when it came to carving. He did a lot of it on those long voyages. I've been reading his old logbook that you returned to me, and in it he mentions his carving more than once. But there are only a few things he made left in the family. I'm glad these have been found."

Susan heard a halting step and looked about in time to see Gene come around a corner of the house. He saw her and stopped. She gestured hurriedly toward the beads in his grandfather's hands.

"I brought them down for you," she said. "Gene—don't mind Adam. You can't blame him for not knowing about your leg and—"

"I don't care what he knows!" Gene broke in. "It doesn't make any difference to me."

He was still angry, and she knew there wasn't anything more she could say. She got up from the steps to leave, and then thought of one more thing that still dissatisfied her.

"You know that pool up there in the woods near your house?" she said.

Gene nodded, but he seemed suddenly alert, perhaps even on guard. "What about it?"

"I told you about seeing a queer sort of face looking up at me from the bottom yesterday—off the end of that log near the bank."

"So what?" Gene said. "Lots of things look like faces in the woods."

"I know. But when I tried to show it to Adam this afternoon, I couldn't find it, and he thought I was just imagining things. Have you ever seen anything like that yourself?"

"I never saw a face around there," the Captain said, "and I know that locality pretty well."

Gene was staring at her in a strange way. "If you saw something that looks like a face, then it's sure to be there still."

"But it's not," Susan said with conviction. "I tried hard to find it again." Then she remembered something else. "When you were living at the house, did you ever see people moving around down by the pool at night carrying lanterns?"

Gene's voice was suddenly tense. "Why would anybody be down there at night?"

"That's what I've been wondering," Susan said. "There were lights in the woods last night. After somebody broke into the house—"

Captain Dan, who had been listening to all this in puzzlement, interrupted. "What do you mean, young lady—about someone breaking in?"

She had forgotten that her third "suspect" had not yet been confronted with what had happened. Certainly his first surprise seemed genuine as she told him the details about the thump in the night and the new scratch on the floor. But he hid his surprise rather quickly, Susan felt. When she had finished, he shook his head soberly.

"Can't figure out what it could have been," he said. There was something odd about his tone, and she had a feeling that he might know more than he meant to reveal. In fact, come to think of it, Captain Dan himself was behaving in a more suspicious manner than had either Gene or Altoona Heath. Susan asked her last question quickly.

"Do you think Sarah Teague really comes back to haunt that house?"

The other two answered promptly and at the same time. The Captain said, "Shucks, no!" and Gene said, "Sure, she does!"

Susan looked from one to the other in bewilderment.

"Did you ever see her, Gene?"

Gene shifted his weight uneasily to take it off his bad leg. Then he said something completely unexpected. "I—I think that face you saw in the pool was Sarah Teague's. That's why you saw it one time and not another."

"Oh, come now, boy, that's bosh!" Captain Dan said. "You've both got imaginations wild as a Hudson Valley thunderstorm. You blow up winds out of nothing."

"But she died in that pool," Gene said. "So why wouldn't she haunt it?" And having made this pronouncement, he turned and went limping off in the direction of uphill and the big rock. Susan and the Captain were left staring at each other. Captain Dan looked a little red in the face.

"What he says about Sarah Teague's drowning in that pond is true enough," he told Susan. "It was a sad accident. She wasn't well when she came to live in her son's house—trouble with her heart, I believe. That day she was out walking when she saw one of her little grandchildren fall into the pool. There was no one else around, and Sarah waded right in to haul her out. She pushed the child to land, and then she must have had a heart attack and fallen down in the shallow water. By the time help came, she was dead—drowned in only a few feet of water."

"Then it *is* a haunted pool!" Susan said softly.

"Oh bosh!" the Captain repeated, sounding cross. "I'm going to have a talk with that grandson of mine for trying to scare you. And maybe I'll have a talk with your Aunt Edith too, if you go trying to scare yourself. I've been around these parts a good many years longer than Gene has, and Sarah Teague has never paid a call on me. By the way —speaking of your Aunt Edith, she hasn't sent her donation over for the firemen's fair yet. You'd better remind her about it so she'll give us some things to sell. And now run along with you, I've got work to do."

The Captain rose a little creakily and went inside. He looked rather old and shaky today, she thought sadly. Not at all like the strong, erect fire chief.

When she climbed the hill again, she went up by way of the Teague house and the pool. She had meant to search the water once more for the strange object that looked like a face. But when she reached the clearing, she changed her mind because someone was there ahead of her.

Gene Foster was out on the log, peering down into the water in such an absorbed manner that he did not hear her at all. She stood watching him for a moment, thinking that he looked rather white-faced and strained. She wondered if the face had reappeared and if he was a little afraid of it.

Then, not wanting him to catch her spying on him, she went quietly away to the Teague house, where she found Adam busily mending the railing on the front porch.

13

The Teague Secret

Iᴛ ᴡᴀs Adam who made an interesting discovery at the Old Oak the following morning. Aunt Edith had gathered up some things that she would give to be sold at the firemen's fair, and she had phoned Captain Dan to ask if he wanted to donate some of the old novels and books of no value that had been packed in the barrel from his attic. He thought the idea a good one, and Aunt Edith had set Susan and Adam to packing all these things into a carton, to be taken up to the firehouse when it was ready.

Susan, in her eagerness to be useful, and in order to show Adam what a good worker she was, picked up more books in one armful than she could manage, and several went flying across the floor, scaring Boneless out of a sound sleep. When she started to pick them up, Adam reached out to stop her.

"Wait a minute," he said. "Here's something odd. Look at the edges of this book."

The book was the old one on English history that Susan had noticed before. It had fallen open on the floor with the pages in a fanned-out position, and there seemed to be some sort of picture painted on the slanting edges.

When Adam picked up the book and closed it, the picture vanished except for a few vague markings. But when he opened the cover and fanned out the edges again, a complete picture appeared. An artist had painted the front of a castle, with a moat and drawbridge and turrets on the very edges of the book, all done in colors now pale and faded.

Susan called her aunt, and Adam showed her the book, first as a closed volume, then with the pages fanned out so that the painting was revealed. "This *is* a find!" Aunt Edith cried. "Fore-edge painting is to be seen every now and then on old books. But this sort of disappearing picture is much more rare. I believe an English bookbinder started doing it a couple of hundred years ago. I must find out if this is of any value. Perhaps it will bring a little more for the Captain than the rest of his books. I *am* glad you discovered it."

After that, Susan and Adam went through every book that had been packed in the Captain's barrel, fanning the pages to see if they could find any more concealed pictures. But no more such volumes came to light.

When the carton was packed, Adam carried it out to the car and went off with Aunt Edith to get it to the firehouse for her. Susan stayed to watch the shop, but she did not return inside at once. Because it was a lovely day, she walked around to the side lawn to view the marble statues once more. To her surprise, she found that the statues had been joined by a visitor. There in the little summerhouse sat Miss Altoona Heath. Today she wore a flowing striped skirt that suited her better, though she still wore the peaked straw hat and sunglasses. At the moment, she was absorbed in studying the lovely marble girl with the lyre in her hands.

As Susan approached, she looked up. "Good morning," she said. "I'm just trying to decide whether or not I can use her."

"Use her?" Susan asked.

"Oh, not in a garden," Miss Altoona assured her, as if that was what Susan had suggested. "I think I'd like her in a corner of my living room. Do you know how much your aunt wants for her?"

Susan did not, but she thought the marble girl rather large for a living room, and she said so.

"Perhaps you're right. I might put her in the hallway on the stairs then. Yes—I do believe that's the place for her." Having made up her mind, she pursed up her mouth at Susan. "When are you coming to see me?" she asked.

Susan had no ready answer. It might be interesting to see Miss Altoona's houseful of treasures,
but at the same time this woman always left her a
little uneasy.

Miss Altoona did not miss her hesitation. "I don't
blame you," she said. "If I were your age, I wouldn't
want to go visiting a funny old woman like me."

Before Susan could think of a reply, Miss Altoona left the summerhouse and went up the steps
of the shop and through the door. Susan followed
her, still feeling rather uncomfortable. Once inside,
the woman strolled around, looking idly at one
thing and another, as if this was a place she enjoyed being in. For the moment she seemed to
have forgotten her invitation, lost in her own
thoughts.

Remembering her interest in the Captain's books,
Susan told her that some of them would be on sale
during the fair, and she showed her the book they
had just found with the painted fore edges.

Miss Altoona seemed mildly interested in this
book for itself, but her original avid desire to look
through the Captain's barrel seemed to have evap-
orated. She merely glanced at those that were left
on the table and shrugged her plump shoulders.

"I don't need that step any more," she said
strangely. "I've been able to move ahead without
it. Though it might be fun to follow up the book
clue just for itself. When I find it, that is. I know
the Teague house almost as well as my own. I used
to play there a lot as a child. But I never could
decide just where—" She broke off suddenly. "I talk

too much, don't I?" she added, and took off her sunglasses to peer at Susan.

A surprisingly young pair of blue eyes seemed to look out of her rather sad old face. A twinge of pity for Miss Altoona tugged at Susan, and she spoke impulsively.

"I'd love to come to see you," she said, and was rewarded by the way Miss Altoona's face lighted up.

"You must come soon, then," she said. "What about tomorrow afternoon at teatime? We'll have a party with fudge cake and limeade and—and lemon drops. I always loved lemon drops when I was your age. Or perhaps a little younger."

"Would you mind if I brought my brother?" Susan asked. She was not at all sure Adam would come, but she wanted company, and the fudge cake might interest him.

Miss Altoona hesitated, as if she did not altogether like the idea of a visit from Adam. Then she nodded.

"Do bring him. I expect he is past the age where he would jump around and break things as little boys do."

Susan assured her that Adam would behave in quite a civilized manner if he came, and Miss Altoona slipped away, leaving word that she would think about purchasing the marble maiden.

It was not until much later in the day, when Susan was back at the Teague house cleaning up for dinner, that she remembered something. There was still one book from the Captain's barrel whose margins she had not examined. She opened a drawer in the highboy and drew out the clipper-ship book. It was a fairly large book, and when the pages were fanned, the thickness would be increased considerably.

She laid the book on her bed and turned back its cover. Then she slanted the fore edges, and at once markings appeared. However, this was no picture. It was clearly a makeshift drawing that someone had attempted with a pen. Though Susan could make nothing at all of the lines and scratches, she felt this was a find, and she took it down the hall to show to Adam.

He had changed from jeans to a good pair of slacks, since Aunt Edith made the same rule Mom did at home—no play clothes at dinnertime. There were occasions, Mom said, when giving other people something pleasant and clean to look at was more important than one's own sloppy comfort. He had showered, and his red hair was slicked down, though already the forelock showed signs of escaping over his right eyebrow.

"Look," Susan said and held out the book.

Adam turned the volume this way and that, trying to make something of the markings on the page edges.

"It looks like a sort of diagram," he said at last. "I wonder if it could be directions for something— a sort of plan or a blueprint? It reminds me of something, only I can't think what."

Susan took another good look at the marks, but

they did not remind her of anything at all. Perhaps the other old book with the fore-edge painting had given someone in the Teague family the idea of using the edges of this book to make a similiar picture. Only it hadn't turned out very well.

"Maybe Captain Dan will know what it means," Susan said.

"Give me time to think about it first," Adam suggested. "Let me keep the book for a little while."

As they went downstairs together, Susan told him about the invitation for tomorrow afternoon from Miss Altoona. Adam made a face but agreed to come with her if they didn't stay too long.

After dinner, Aunt Edith took them for a drive through West Point and up a bit farther along the river. They returned fairly late, and Susan went right to bed.

Now that Adam was sleeping on the same floor, she no longer lay awake listening to the sounds of the night, or to the creaking of the house. Indeed, she heardly heard the boats on the river any more, or the trains running along its bank. That night she fell asleep thinking of the river flowing past so quietly out there in the darkness. It was strange about the Hudson—even when she could not see it, she had a feeling of its being part of the everyday life of these towns along its edge. The river was a highway to the sea, and a barrier at the same time, giving them glimpses only of what seemed practically another country over on the east side.

Mostly she did not even hear the cuckoo clock any more, when it called the hours of the night.

Nevertheless, she must have had some sort of warning sixth sense at work, for quite suddenly in the night she wakened with the feeling that once more someone was moving stealthily about the house.

Because of Adam's presence she was not frightened this time. She got out of bed and went boldly to the stairs and listened. The sounds were very soft, but she could hear them somewhere below. Perhaps it was only Mrs. Bancroft up for a late snack. She didn't want to call Adam and then look silly if it was nothing, so she tiptoed softly down the third-floor stairs and stole to the railing of the balcony that overlooked the living room.

At once she saw a light moving about below. Someone with a flashlight was throwing the beam along the walls, across pictures, over the fireplace and the mirrors at either side. She dared not go back to call Adam now and give the intruder the alarm. First she must know once and for all who it was that stole into this house in the dead of night.

Her finger found the light switch near the stairs, and the living room flashed into view like a suddenly illuminated picture. A boy in pajamas knelt before the fireplace. Startled by the light, he turned and saw her watching him from the balcony above. It was Adam.

"Turn off that light!" he whispered urgently. "Why couldn't you stay in bed? Now you'll have everybody awake."

"Nobody's awake but us," Susan whispered back. "What in the world are you doing?"

"Now that you're up, come down here and help

me," Adam ordered. "I remembered what that diagram reminded me of and came down here to see if I was right."

Susan turned off the light and felt her way down the stairs. With the beam of his flashlight, Adam showed her the pen markings on the page edges of the book he had brought down with him.

"Look here—doesn't that square look like one of the panels at the side of the fireplace? The one with the mirror above it on the left side. And couldn't that square box with the straight line over it be meant for the fireplace and the mantel? This looks like an arrow here, and another one pointing there. I'm sure of it!"

As his finger indicated these things, she could see them for herself.

"But what do the marks mean?" she pondered.

"That's what I'm trying to figure out. Hold the flashlight for me, and let's see what I can find."

While Susan played the beam on a mahogany panel low on the wall beside the fireplace, Adam began to feel along the raised wood of its sides. He pressed and pulled and tugged and patted at the place that one of the arrows in the drawing seemed to indicate.

"There's something loose here," he whispered to his sister in triumph. "Something's moving!"

As Susan watched, one of the amall squares in the panel slid outward at the pressure of Adam's fingers, leaving a dark aperture behind. The opening was no larger than a cereal box, and when Adam reached into it he found nothing there.

"It feels empty," he said. "Bring the light closer."

Susan knelt beside him in order to shine the flashlight into the small opening. There was clearly nothing there.

"What do you suppose was hidden in there?" Susan asked.

"I'm not sure anything was hidden here," Adam told her. "I don't think that's what it was meant for. There's an arrow that seems to point up inside the opening."

He put his hand into the opening and pushed at its walls and ceiling. There was a faint creaking sound, and the ceiling panel of the little space lifted upward and back as if it was hinged. Adam put his hand through the new opening, and his arm followed it up to the shoulder. He looked at his sister in excitement.

"There's a big hidden compartment above this little one. It's so big I can't find the top. Wait a minute—I can feel a knob of some sort near the front wall. Watch and see if anything happens when I move it."

Susan flashed the beam upward and it shone back at her from the long mirror set into the wall. As she watched, the mirror began to slide sideways slowly, slowly, disappearing into the wall, and as it moved, the alcove behind came into full view.

"Look!" Susan cried softly.

Adam gave the knob a last turn and stood up to view the opening that was now visible to the room. This alcove was far from small. A great space several feet high and quite deep had been built into the wall. If Rufus Teague's son had built this house, then he must have designed this hiding place when the house was planned. It did not seem like anything that could have been added later. But if this was the secret, then it was far from satisfactory. The hidden alcove stood revealed, yes—but it stood quite empty of the slightest adornment. If anything had ever been concealed in this place, it was gone now.

Adam stared at the cavernous opening, as puzzled as Susan. "It's hard to figure out what anybody would keep in a place like that. It's almost big enough to hide a man, if he sat down and pulled up his knees."

Susan played the light over the alcove, then over the fireplace and the panels on either side. No answer was revealed. She sent the finger of light sliding across the floor to where a rug hid the long scratch.

"I think I know now," she said. "Whatever was hidden up there was taken out the first night Aunt Edith and I moved into this house. I think it was dragged across the floor and made that scratch."

"Maybe you're right," Adam conceded. "In that case it must have been Captain Dan or his grandson who did the moving. Since I don't think it was the Captain, it must have been Gene."

"But why?" Susan asked, completely baffled. "If Gene wanted something taken out of that hiding place, he could have just taken it openly. What could it be that he would want to hide from us? It doesn't make sense."

"The thing I can't figure out," Adam said, "is what would need that much room to hide. It all seems sort of crazy."

"Besides, if it were that big, it would probably be heavy," Susan mused. "So I don't see how Gene could get it down."

"Unless he wasn't alone," Adam said. "Anyway, I'd better close the mirror panel for now so we can go back to bed."

Once more he moved the knob in the upper compartment, and the mirror slid back into place, an integral part of the wall.

"Even if that mirror were broken, you wouldn't find the hiding place," Adam said, "because it's set against a backing that looks like part of the wall."

As they started upstairs together, Adam took the flashlight and led the way. When they reached the third floor, he spoke again in a whisper.

"Let's keep quiet about this. Maybe we can find out more about it if we don't tell what we know right away."

Susan agreed willingly. She had still another reason for saying nothing. Somehow she did not want to give away this secret that the Teagues had kept for so long, and she had an idea that Gene would never forgive her if she did.

When she was back in her own room and in bed again, Susan puzzled further about their discovery. Now she could guess why Gene was worried about those books leaving the house. He must have known that some such diagram existed which would show how to open the panels. He must have known it was in an old book. Since he and his grandfather knew the secret themselves, they didn't need the book to give them directions, but Gene hadn't wanted it to fall into other hands.

This must have been the reason why Miss Altoona had been interested in the books in the beginning. Stories must have been passed around for years. But now that Miss Altoona was no longer interested in the key to the hidden compartment, did that mean—? No! Susan put the thought out of her mind. She couldn't imagine the plump Miss Altoona Heath breaking into a house to open the secret compartment and get something heavy out of it. She didn't see how Gene could have managed it either. And she couldn't believe it had been the Captain. So where were they—now that she and Adam had discovered the "secret"?

14

The Face Again

THE NEXT DAY Adam made friends with the people who ran the boathouse and lived in the clubhouse down on the dock. He spent the morning chugging happily up and down the river with their son, who was a few years older than himself. Susan wasn't invited and she didn't mind. The only time she had been in a motorboat it had leaped and banged the water so hard that she had disliked the jarring ride.

At least Adam was ready to settle down to something less active when he came home for their date with Miss Altoona. He grumbled about going but cleaned up in time and accompanied Susan to the Heath mansion.

Miss Altoona employed several servants. They saw a gardener working outside, and a maid came to the door to invite them in. Their hostess, dressed in a fluttery green gown, and for once without straw hat and sunglasses, came to greet them with so much pleasure that Susan felt a little guilty about some of her own thoughts. Since Miss Altoona was so glad to entertain two young people, it was probable that no one came to see her very often.

The main hallway of the house was long, running from the front to the back, but it was fairly narrow, and Susan, thinking of the marble girl Miss Altoona wanted to buy, wondered where she had meant to put it. Her hostess must have guessed her thoughts, for she waved a hand toward the stair landing.

"If I buy your aunt's marble maiden, I'll put her right up there. She can have the whole landing to herself and play her lyre for me whenever I go by. This is your brother, isn't it? I'm glad to meet you, Adam. Do come into the drawing room, both of you."

She moved ahead, her green draperies fluttering around her. A mingling of odors met Susan's nose as she entered the big room—a musty smell, mixed with mothballs, as if the room had not been opened for guests for a long while. A fire was burning in the grate, in spite of the warm day.

"I do like a fire when I have company," Miss Altoona said. "It looks so cheerful."

Since they all sat near open windows, the heat didn't matter too much. Susan looked around the room with interest. It was furnished—or perhaps "cluttered" was the word—with everything possible in the way of furniture and curios. It might easily have been the showroom of a shop like Aunt Edith's, except that there seemed to be a good many things from the Orient rubbing elbows with American antiques. A Chinese screen stood on a hooked rug, and there were various other mixtures.

Miss Altoona rang a brass temple bell, and almost at once refreshments arrived—tall glasses of limeade, small sandwiches that made about a mouthful each, and the promised fudge cake. While Susan and her brother ate, their hostess, who said she was on a diet, nibbled chocolate frosting and told them about some of the objects she liked best in the room.

"I love things from distant countries," she said. "How I wish I could travel around the world and see all the places they come from!"

"Why don't you?" Adam asked, and Susan suspected that he thought her a little silly.

The question seemed to startle Miss Altoona. "But I've never traveled anywhere. I wouldn't know the first thing about how to do it."

"Finding out can't be so hard," Adam said. He was beginning to look a little bored, and Susan decided that she had better do something to distract him.

She set her plate on a table and went across the room to examine a beautiful little jade Buddha. This drew Miss Altoona out of her chair and set them all stirring about the room on a sort of conducted tour. Adam on the move was not apt to be as restless as Adam sitting still.

At the end of the room, opposite the fireplace, was a pair of double doors with handsomely carved wooden panels. Miss Altoona paused before them and turned a china knob, pushing open one of the doors.

"This was my father's library," she said. "He

never liked me to come in here, so I didn't read very much as a child."

Susan looked into a room that was dim except for a bar of light slanting through one partly opened shutter. At that moment a telephone rang in the hall, and Miss Altoona jumped nervously.

"Do excuse me," she said. "That must be my call from New York!"—and away she rushed to answer the phone.

Susan looked at Adam pleadingly. "We don't have to stay very long, so do be nice. I can't help feeling sorry for her."

"I think she's bats," Adam said. He stepped through the open door of the library and looked about, while Susan examined the nearest row of bookshelves.

Again there was the musty smell of a place seldom aired, mingling with the odors of furniture polish and dusty draperies. Susan took down a book and sneezed as she stirred the dust from its neglected leaves. From the direction of the hall she could hear the mumble of Miss Altoona's voice.

"Hey!" Adam said suddenly. "What do you think this is?"

He was standing beside a black leather armchair, peering behind it into a dark corner. Susan joined him and looked over the back of the chair. What she saw startled her so much that she gripped Adam's arm.

A face was staring at them from behind the chair. The neck seemed to arch back as if the thing had raised its head to look up at them out of the gloom. The eyes were lost in dark sockets, the mouth set in a forbidding line. It was a head with neck and shoulders, but no body—a huge face, larger than life-size.

"There—she's hung up the phone," Adam whispered, and with unspoken agreement they moved quickly away from the strange object hidden in the room's darkest corner and returned to the door.

Miss Altoona rejoined them a little out of breath, her cheeks pink as if with excitement.

"That was a dealer from New York," she explained, sounding elated and triumphant. "I asked him to confirm something I had already suspected. It was good news, very good news indeed."

She laughed softly and then became aware of her guests' blank looks.

"I'm sorry," she said, "but I can't explain just now. I am really going to have a surprise for your Aunt Edith one of these days."

Then she seemed to remember where she had left Susan and Adam while she went to answer the phone. Her blue eyes narrowed, and she looked from one to the other, as if she were searching for some sign. Susan tried to keep her face expressionless, and Adam looked bored again. Apparently satisfied that they had noticed nothing, she led them back into the drawing room.

But now Susan knew that Miss Altoona was hiding something. She still tingled with a sense of recognition of the face that had stared at her from behind the chair in the library. It was the same face she had seen blurred and wavery, beneath the waters of the woodland pool. There was no mistake—she would never forget it.

She could hardly wait to get away where she could talk to Adam. It was a relief when they were able to thank Miss Altoona and say good-bye. She saw them to the door, and the two set off through the section back of the lake, moving toward the Teague house. Adam had not missed his sister's suppressed excitement.

"What are you simmering about?" he asked.

"It was that face!" Susan cried. "Do you know what it was?"

"It looked like some sort of wooden statue—or at least the head and shoulders of a statue."

"It was the face I saw in the pool!" Susan told him. "I'd know it anywhere. There really *was* a face in the water, and I wasn't dreaming."

Adam thought about this as they walked along in silence.

"But it doesn't make any sense that somebody would dump that head into a pool," he said after a while.

Susan had been pondering that too. "What if it were just hidden there temporarily?"

"On the way from where to where?" Adam sounded unbelieving.

"Maybe from Captain Dan's house?"

Adam stood still on the road and stared at her. "You could be right, at that."

"It would fit, wouldn't it?" Susan asked.

Adam knew what she meant. "Fit the secret alcove, you mean? Yes, I should think it would be just about the right size. It was a lot bigger than a real head."

"So maybe it *was* Miss Altoona Sunday night," Susan went on. "Maybe she found out about the hiding place and took the head. But it was too hard for her to manage, so she hid it in the pool. Then she came back with help the next night—when I saw lanterns in the woods—and got it up to her house."

"If that's it, then we ought to report this to Captain Dan," Adam said.

He started to walk again, and Susan moved quickly along beside him. "Couldn't we wait a little while?" she pleaded. "There's still something awfully queer about all this. Why would anybody put anything as ugly as that head in a secret hiding place?"

"I don't know," Adam said. "It seemed a strange sort of face, but a strong one. I'm not sure I'd call it ugly. Could you tell whether it represented a man or a woman?"

Susan walked along without answering at once. She was trying intently to bring back the details of the face she had glimpsed so briefly, hidden there in the shadows of the dark library. The hair had been visible, combed back from a wide brow. It had been a brownish color like the rest of the wood from which the head was made, but she did not know whether it was the hair of a man or a woman. However, there must be some other detail that would give her the answer if she could only remember it. She could almost see it in her mind. Something about the neck of the figure. Had there been a man's collar or the neck of a woman's dress showing? She could not remember.

Because there was something she felt she ought to recall, she was a little absentminded all through dinner, and afterward. Aunt Edith tried to draw her out, but she wasn't ready to tell the whole story yet. Once this was launched into the hands of adults, all sorts of unpleasant things might happen. Some of them to Miss Altoona. And in spite of what had happened, Susan's feeling of sympathy and pity for that rather odd lady was increasing. Of course, she and Adam would have to reveal their discoveries sooner or later. But as Adam had said, the first person they ought to tell was Captain Dan.

It wasn't until Susan was undressing for bed that night that the detail which had escaped her suddenly returned to her mind. The head in the library *had* been that of a woman. She knew because there had been a string of large beads about the throat. Beads of a sort she had seen before. They were like those Captain Rufus Teague had carved long ago, which she had taken down to the cabin to give to Gene.

She sat on the edge of her bed with one shoe off, thinking for a long time. Did that mean that this wooden face, or head, had been carved long ago by Rufus Teague? Was it perhaps a work of art, and thus rather valuable? Was that why Altoona Heath wanted it? But she must have known she couldn't just take it out of the Captain's house and get away with such an action. Even a person with her odd notions would know that.

Whatever road they took, Susan's thoughts led to confusion and to puzzles she could not answer. Yet every question came back to the mystery of why the son of Captain Rufus Teague had built a secret compartment in his house and had hidden that head carved by his father (if it had been carved by him) away from the sight of all except the family. And why had the other Teagues since that time held to the same custom, hiding the strange carved face from view?

It was quite a while before Susan took her other shoe off and finally got into bed. No sooner did her head touch the pillow, however, than another memory came to her. Glimpsing that face today, more clearly than she had through the waters of the pond, had given her a feeling that she had seen it before somewhere, that it was familiar to her in still another way. And now she knew why.

Slipping out of bed, she took the book about clipper ships from its drawer and brought it back to the reading lamp beside her bed. Quickly she turned the pages, looking, looking. Yes, there it was—that old photograph that had been taken of Rufus Teague and his wife, Sarah. And there was the face for which she searched.

The huge carved head had been a portrait in a sense. A portrait Rufus Teague must have made of Sarah. The woman who sat beside him had the same strong face, the same deep eye sockets and forbidding mouth.

Susan shivered and closed the pages. That face, she was sure, was going to haunt her memory for a long time.

15

Storm Over the Hudson

THE NEXT DAY was Friday—the day before the firemen's fair. From the beginning it was hot and sultry. Not a breeze ruffled the surface of the Hudson. A few puffy white clouds seemed to hang suspended in the northern distance without moving at all.

"Thunder weather," Aunt Edith said at breakfast. "You'd better not stir very far—I think it's going to storm. Oh, I do hope it will be clear for the fair tomorrow. You've no idea how important our volunteer company is to Highland Crossing. Ten years ago we had to rely on the next town for help, and there was always a delay about getting the engines here. Now, thanks to Captain Dan's organizing of our company and the fine training given all the men, we can go to sleep at night without the worry we used to have. Of course, Captain Dan is sure to be re-elected tomorrow as chief."

"You mean they take a vote tomorrow?" Adam asked, helping himself to Mrs. Bancroft's home-made strawberry jam.

"That's right. It has been the custom ever since the beginning for all the firemen to go inside and take a secret vote with the blackball box at the end of the fair. I don't think one of them would give Captain Dan a blackball, however."

"I haven't met him yet, but if he's Gene's grand-father, isn't he a little old for that job?" Adam asked.

Susan cried, "Oh no!" and Aunt Edith looked a little surprised.

"I never think of Captain Dan as getting older," she said. "He's been the same as long as I re-member, and I'm sure he's as fit as many much younger men. No, I don't think his years will stop him yet."

Because of the threatening, sticky weather, Susan and Adam went to the Old Oak and stayed inside all morning. Aunt Edith had things they could help her with in the shop. Adam put up a new display shelf, and Susan sorted articles for a special sale counter of kitchen utensils. There would be people coming from all around for the fair, and during the day some of them might cross the highway and walk up to the Old Oak to see what was new.

By afternoon the weather had not changed at all, so Aunt Edith told them to go out of doors anyway but not to wander too far off. These Hudson River thunderstorms could break suddenly, almost without warning, and they might be caught in a real downpour.

Susan exchanged a quick, questioning look with her brother, and he nodded. This, she knew, meant that they could go down to see Captain Dan this afternoon and tell him what they had discovered. Together they set off to get the clipper-ship book, and then started down through the woods.

Adam heard the rumble of thunder on the way down and called to Susan to hurry. She looked up and saw that the sky had darkened. The harmless white clouds were no longer distant, and they had turned an ominous black. Even as she hurried after her brother, the rain broke.

They were nearing the cabin, and they started to run, reaching the little porch with cold drops pelting their backs. Around them the woods flashed with green light, and thunder boomed. The sultry stillness was gone, and the air turned sharply cold. Thunder rolled again, crashing from cliff to cliff back and forth across the river in echoing reverberations. Adam knocked loudly on the cabin door, and Captain Dan came to let them in.

"Hello, there," he said, smiling a welcome. "This is just the right day for visitors. Come in out of the storm. I don't believe I've met your brother yet, Susan, though Gene has told me about him."

As they entered the cabin, Susan saw Gene lying on his stomach on a bunk bed across the room, reading a book. He looked up and stared at them distantly, and she wondered what he had told his grandfather about Adam.

The cabin's main room was a good size and comfortably furnished with some of the overflow from the big house. It was a cheerful, rustic room, with an Indian rug before the fireplace and another one hanging against the log wall. The cabin was equipped with electricity and a telephone, but the place must seem small to two people who were accustomed to the spacious house up the hill. It could not have been easy for them to move out of the big house and into this.

Captain Dan suggested that he phone Aunt Edith to let her know they were out of the storm. When that had been done, he began to busy himself at the fireplace. Lightning flared against the windows and thunder shivered the panes of glass as he worked.

"It's turning cool," he said, "and there's nothing like a fire in the grate with a storm outside. This is a good afternoon for popping corn, Gene. How about digging out the popper, boy, and opening a package of corn?"

Thus prodded, Gene sat up on the bunk and closed his book reluctantly. Susan and Adam watched with interest as Captain Dan lighted kindling to start the log fire in the fireplace. It was wonderfully cozy sitting cross-legged on the Indian rug, with rain streaming against the panes and the sound of thunder booming along the hills. Gene and Adam took turns holding the long-handled popper over the fire as the yellow kernels of corn began to explode into puffs of white. When the mound of popcorn grew high in the green bowl Susan had brought from the tiny kitchen, the Captain dropped in a lump of butter and a sprinkling of salt and handed Susan a wooden spoon for stirring.

The feeling of warmth and comfort and companionship penetrated even Gene's guard, and he became a little less stiff and unwelcoming.

It was the sort of day when stories would be told round the fire, and it seemed quite natural when Captain Dan began a yarn about the sea. He told them one of the adventures he had read in the logbook of Captain Rufus Teague, and his listeners heard him through breathlessly.

On that occasion, the *Flying Sarah* had sailed through a typhoon in the Pacific. Even though he had been merely setting down the facts, the color and excitement had come through Rufus Teague's words, and Captain Dan transferred the feeling to his listeners.

When the story was told, and Gene was popping more corn, Susan carried the book she had brought to the Captain's chair and opened it to the picture of Rufus and his wife, Sarah.

"This was in that book barrel too," she said. "It's a book you'll want to keep. There's quite a lot about Captain Rufus and his wife in it."

Gene handed the popper to Adam and came to look over his grandfather's shoulder.

"That carved head looks just like the picture of Sarah Teague," Susan said softly. There!—it was out, though she hadn't waited for Adam's signal.

Both Gene and Captain Dan looked at her quickly. Even Adam stared, because she had not told him of this discovery. The Captain raised shaggy gray eyebrows in a question.

"So you've seen the head that Captain Rufus carved? That means you've found the secret compartment, I suppose?"

"Adam found it," Susan said. "Tell him how."

Adam showed the Captain and Gene the diagram on the page edges of the book, and told how he had gone downstairs at night to search, and how Susan had joined him and together they had opened the sliding panel. But, to Susan's surprise, there was one thing he left out. He said nothing about the fact that the compartment, when they found it, had been empty. In fact, he dropped the story so deliberately at this point that Susan knew he meant to hold back awhile longer the fact that Altoona had the head in her possession. Perhaps he wanted to give Altoona a chance to explain before he told the Captain what she had done. Adam could be surprisingly generous sometimes —when he happened to think of it.

To cover the gap in the story, Susan began to ask questions.

"Why did Captain Rufus make the head so large?" she asked. "It's too big to set up somewhere as an ornament."

Gene uttered his favorite snorting sound. "It wasn't meant as an ornament for inside a house! Don't you know what it was?"

Susan shook her head, helping herself to a fresh handful of hot popcorn.

Gene reached past his grandfather's shoulder and turned back a few pages of the book to the full picture of Captain Rufus' ship, the *Flying Sarah*. "There you are," he said.

Puzzled, Susan stared at the picture. The ship was handsome, as the artist had depicted her under full sail, with a bone between her teeth, as they said of the white curl of waves parting at her prow. Adam looked too, and it was he who saw what Gene meant. He put a finger on the page.

"Don't you see, Susan? *There* is the head!"

He was pointing to the figurehead of the ship. In this picture of the entire ship it was small, but Susan could see that it had been carved in the full-length form of a woman. She stood as if striding out across the very waves, with one foot ahead of the other on the carved base, her full skirt blowing backward in the wind. Her neck was arched so she could look out toward distant seas. There was a grace and sense of speed in the carved figure that matched the grace and speed of the ship and seemed an integral part of it. In profile, the tiny face in the picture was that of the carved head Susan knew well by now.

Captain Dan nodded. "The *Flying Sarah* in full sail. What a ship she must have been! They knew how to build a ship in those days. Captain Rufus was no professional carver of figureheads, but they said this one matched the best of his day. It's probably quite valuable now."

He turned the page to the sketches of various details of the ship, and the figurehead was there again, shown a bit larger than in the first picture. Again it was in profile, and not easily recognizable to someone who had seen the head only in full face.

Susan studied the picture thoughtfully. "There's one thing missing," she said. "The real carved head has a string of beads around the throat. Beads just like the ones I brought down to you the other day. But there aren't any beads in this picture."

"You have a sharp eye, girl," Captain Dan said. "And you're right, of course. But those beads were added to the figurehead later on. Old Rufus knew how fond his wife was of the first beads he had carved for her, and he wanted the figurehead to look exactly like her. So on that last voyage he carved a set especially for the figure."

Gene moved restlessly, as if he was uneasy. After hardly more than a glance at the pictures, he had gone to stand at a window, where he could look out at the slanting rain.

The wind had risen, and they could hear the trees threshing shaggy branches overhead. The little cabin shivered in sudden fierce gusts, but it stood firm and sound against the impact.

Without warning, brilliant lightning flared, and a deafening clap of thunder shattered the air. Gene winced and moved back from the window.

"That was close!" he said. "Just up the hill, I think."

Susan had put her hands over her ears. If it was near, she hoped lightning hadn't struck the Teague house or her aunt's shop.

It was not the storm, however, that held Gene's main interest. He was looking at his grandfather.

"How do you know about the beads?" he asked. "How do you know he made them for the figurehead that last voyage?"

The Captain tapped the logbook on the table beside him. "Your great-great-great-grandfather tells right here about carving that second strand of beads. He was working on them all through that long voyage, and he mentions them in the last entry he made before the ship went into pirate waters. He never wrote in his log again after that. Here's the entry."

The room was very still. There had been no second clap of thunder as loud as the last. The storm had done its worst and was abating. Gene stood with his back to the window, where rain still whispered against the pane. Adam sat on the Indian rug beside the bowl of popcorn, and Susan stopped chewing to listen. The Captain turned the yellowing pages of the log until he found the place he wanted. Then he began to read aloud.

"The beads are finished, and a fine set they are.

I've done better work on these than on my first. The figurehead can wear them for a while—to dress her up a bit. I'll climb out over the bowsprit and fasten them on her shortly. But I'll not leave them to her. Work like this is not to be wasted around the neck of even so fine a wooden figure."

"That's all he wrote," Captain Dan said. "That was his last entry. He must have put those beads around the figurehead's neck right after he wrote in the book. But he wasn't there to take them off at the end of the voyage. So there they've stayed, just where he put them, the way the real Sarah wore her beads so lovingly all her life."

A thoughtful quiet fell upon the room. Susan was thinking sadly of Captain Rufus, who had been a brave sailor and who had died with his men in the fighting that was to come after he had written those words. The fire glowed into embers, but the Captain, lost in a reverie of his own, made no move to replenish it. Outside, a glint of sunshine shone at a window, reflecting in the raindrops. It was clearing now.

Gene spoke urgently to Adam and Susan.

"Don't tell anybody about the secret hiding place! Nobody but Teagues have known about it for all this time. If we hadn't let you into our house, you wouldn't have known either. So it's not your secret to tell."

"Maybe it is theirs at that," Captain Dan said gently. "Or will be. You might as well know my plans, Gene. If the Prices and Edith Sperry want to buy, then I'm going to sell. I'd rather they had the house than somebody else."

"You'll hate giving it up!" Gene protested, and there was both misery and anger in his eyes. "It's our home. You love it the way I do. We can't live the year round in a shack like this!"

"We can and we will," the Captain said, but Susan heard the sadness in his voice and knew that Gene spoke the truth. It would hurt Captain Dan deeply to give up his home. But he had made up his mind.

"There's nothing else to do, boy," he added. "You know that."

"Because of me!" Gene said bitterly. "It's all because of me that we have to lose the house!"

The Captain spoke more sharply than Susan had ever heard him. "It's a weak, useless thing to cry over spilt milk. When a thing's done, a man goes on from there and does what he has to do. He doesn't keep blaming himself for what's past, when blame won't help. It's only what he does today and in the future that matters." He set the logbook aside and rose from his chair. "The rain's over. I'm going out to see if there's been any wind damage. Susan, you and Adam stay as long as you like. You're welcome here."

No one said anything as he went out of the cabin. Susan could not bear to look at Gene. Adam got up and moved around the room as if he could not sit still another minute. In one corner he came upon Gene's fishing pole and examined it with interest.

"I'd sure like to go fishing one of these days," he said.

Gene made no response. It was as if he had not heard. Susan was relieved when Adam started toward the door.

"Guess we'd better get home," he said.

Gene took a limping step toward him. "Wait a minute! Tell me first where you saw that carved head. You saw in the pond, didn't you, Susan? And then where? Tell me where it is now!"

At his tone of command, Adam showed signs of bristling, but Susan spoke quickly before there could be sharp words between them.

"Miss Altoona has it. We saw it in the library of her house yesterday."

"So that's it!" Gene sounded grim. "Grandfather doesn't know it's gone, and I don't want him to find out. I'm going up to talk to Miss Altoona right now. That carving is valuable family property, and to her, it's just another antique."

Perhaps it had been about the figurehead that Miss Altoona had been phoning that dealer in New York, Susan thought. "But how could she possibly think she had a right to keep what belonged to the Teagues?"

Adam had begun to look interested in the promise of action. "I don't think she'll give it up easily," he told Gene. "Maybe I'd better come along and help."

"I don't need your help," Gene said stiffly.

"I'm coming anyway," said Adam.

Gene went out of the cabin without answering, and Adam followed him. Not to be left behind when something exciting was about to happen, Susan hurried after the two boys.

There was a side road farther on, and when Gene headed for it, Adam and Susan followed.

16

The Siren Blows

THE BOYS walked ahead, Gene determined enough to manage a fair pace in spite of his limp. Susan trailed a little way behind, her thoughts in a state of confusion. Now that she knew the strange face had been part of a figurehead on a ship, much was cleared up that had puzzled her. But there were still unanswered questions. She still did not know why the head had been concealed in a secret compartment all these years. And she certainly didn't know how or why it had been moved from that compartment into the pond, and then into the house of Altoona Heath. Nor did she understand why Gene was so anxious to hide from his grandfather the fact that Miss Altoona had the head.

All around the woods were dripping, and every leaf was ashine with diamond drops of rain. A wet branch slapped back at Susan as one of the boys released it. The air was cool and tangy with a smell of earth and growing things.

The sudden, earsplitting wail startled Susan, and she stopped in dismay to listen. That was the siren on top of the firehouse. Gene, who had reached the road ahead, stopped, too, and looked

back undecidedly toward his grandfather's cabin.
Susan knew he must be debating whether to go
on or to turn back to join his grandfather.

"Come along!" Adam called in high excitement.
"I can smell smoke. I think the fire's nearby."

"If it is," Gene said, "then you don't belong there,
getting in the way. You'd better go home. Both of
you."

Adam, however, was not Aunt Edith when it
came to listening to reason.

"You aren't the chief," he told Gene, and hurried on along the road, excitement showing in his
step.

The other boy offered no further argument, and
they went on as fast as Gene could manage with
the brace on his leg. Susan kept up with them now.
She wasn't going to be left behind. The breeze carried a smell of smoke, and she could hear the crackle
of flames. The fire was close.

A car went by, beeping its horn, and Susan saw
Captain Dan at the wheel. He was the fire chief
now as he hurried toward headquarters to take
charge. Gene made no attempt to flag him down.
A delay would be against the rules.

As they reached the paved road that ran back
of the lake, he pointed. The burning house was in
clear view, and it was one Susan recognized—
the house of Altoona Heath. A portion of the roof
was on fire, its shingles burning in lively fashion,
and flames were creeping downward beneath the
eaves at one corner.

"That's where the lightning must have struck," Gene said. "She didn't find it right away and it's got a head start."

Adam began to run in the direction of the fire, excitement urging him on, and Gene could no longer keep up with him. Susan wanted to run too, but she hadn't the heart to leave Gene, who was already struggling to move as quickly as he could.

Poor Miss Altoona! Where was she? Did she know that all her treasures might burn, and the figurehead with them?

"Do you think it's bad?" she asked Gene, panting, as they came up in front of the house. "Will the whole house go?"

"Depends on what's happening inside," Gene said. "There—the fire engines are starting up."

Miss Altoona and her servants came running around from the side of the house, Altoona wringing her hands wildly.

"All my beautiful things!" she wailed. "I'm going to lose everything—everything!" There had been no time to reach for her hat and sunglasses, so she looked like almost anyone today. Gene and Adam went to stand beside her, watching the fire, and Susan could see that Adam was eager to edge as close to the danger line as he dared.

"It's a good thing the figurehead is downstairs in the library," Gene said. "They ought to get the flames out before the fire reaches that."

Miss Altoona heard him and started sobbing anew. "It's *not* in the library! It will burn too, along with everything else. Last night I had it taken up to the attic where I could—could keep it hidden. It's there now, right where the fire is burning."

Gene turned quite pale. "Then if it burns it will be my fault. I got it out of our house with a rope-and-pulley contraption I worked out. But I couldn't drag it very far through the woods, so I pushed it into the pond until I could find a good place to hide it. I figured a few days of water wouldn't hurt something that had sailed the oceans on a ship." He turned angrily upon Miss Altoona. "Why couldn't you leave it alone? Why did you have to steal it?"

Miss Altoona paused in the middle of a loud cry of anguish and looked at him indignantly. "It wasn't stealing. I heard Susan say she had seen a face in the pond, and I went to look. Nobody can blame me for getting my gardener down there to haul out something that had been dumped into a pond—just thrown away. Oh dear, oh dear, everything is going to burn!"

Adam looked from one to the other, and Susan could see that his rising state of excitement was urging him into action. Before she could say anything, he spoke to Gene.

"I'll go in and get the figurehead," he told him. "I'll go upstairs and bring that carving out if it's valuable to your grandfather."

Gene grabbed him by the arm. "Don't be foolish. No one goes into a burning house to save anything but a life. The smoke's all through the attic by now—you'd never make it. Here come the engines anyway."

But Adam had clearly been seized by the notion of playing the hero and pitting his own wits and strength against the fire. He threw off Gene's grasping hand and started toward the steps just as the fire engines and the chief's car came roaring around the turn in the road. In a moment Adam would have been inside the house ahead of the firemen, racing for the attic. But in that instant Gene did a most astonishing thing. He threw himself into the air, diving for Adam in an amazing flying tackle, and brought him down upon the grass with a thud, his arms clasped around Adam's legs. Both boys rolled outstretched on the ground, and Gene hung on with all his might.

The chief jumped out of his car, giving orders as he came. His white helmet shone in the sunlight, in contrast to the black helmets of the volunteers, as they leaped from the fire engines and jumped out of their private cars. Two men in smoke masks ran past Susan with axes and pike poles in their hands. The men in charge of the fire lines began clearing everyone back from the lawn to the other side of the road. Already spectators were crowding around, tripping over hose, getting in the way. The fire-line men worked quickly, expertly, ordering them back, halting cars, keeping the road free.

The men in masks had gone inside. Others lined

up an extension ladder against the roof. More hose was swiftly uncoiled from the crib on top of the engine, attached to the water source, and in a moment men were aiming powerful streams against the roof. There was a great hissing of steam as water struck the flames broadside. For an instant the fire seemed to retreat from the water. Then it flared out again, more ravenous than ever.

On the ground below, the chief shouted orders through the bull horn that magnified his voice so that it could be heard above the uproar.

Susan found that she had somehow been pushed back out of harm's way across the road, with Miss Altoona beside her, still wringing her hands. She looked about for her brother, and saw that Adam was helping Gene to the chief's car in a surprisingly solicitous way. Gene limped worse than before, as if he might have hurt his bad leg. At the same time he was grinning broadly, and Susan thought she knew why. Handicapped though he was, Gene had proved that he could stop a perfectly able-bodied boy from doing a reckless and foolish thing. It was possible that Adam owed his life to Gene Foster's good sense and courage.

The crash of breaking glass from attic windows added to the turmoil of shouting and the roar of the flames, which had sprung up in a new place on the roof.

There was a horrid smell of burning in the air and a fine drifting of cinders on the slight breeze. What a good thing that no strong wind was blowing and that things were still wet after the rain! Susan could taste the acrid odors on her tongue, as if tasting and smelling were the same thing. Beside her, Miss Altoona had gone limp and was leaning rather heavily on Susan's shoulder. She had stopped her wailing and now watched the scene before her with dazed eyes.

More men with axes and pike poles had gone inside the house, and you could see them at the attic windows where glass had been broken out. Smoke was pouring out thickly from one portion of the attic, and as Susan watched, two men came downstairs and out the front door, carrying a limp comrade between them. They laid him on the grass, and at once two other volunteers came over with an oxygen mask and placed it over his face. Gene had said smoke poisoning could hit you before you knew what was happening. If Adam had gone up there alone—!

Then the effect of seeming turmoil and confusion began to die down. No more flames leaped hungrily from the roof. The clouds of smoke were thinning to a wet, gray vapor. The crowding spectators began to get into their cars and drive away, though immediate neighbors remained to watch a while longer. Miss Altoona and her servants and Susan were permitted to move back to the wet lawn of the house. The chief had gone over to his car to speak to Gene and Adam, and now he approached Miss Altoona, his boots squishing on the wet ground.

"The fire's been extinguished, and all hands are securing," he told her. "That lightning bolt must have struck the roof. You'll have some roof repairs to make, and there's some water damage up there too. But not too much on the floors below. Things look pretty good, considering."

Miss Altoona gulped and looked as if she might cry again. The chief went on quickly, soberly.

"I don't understand just how it happened, but my grandson tells me there's a piece of our property up there in your attic. Something you, uh, borrowed under unusual circumstances."

Miss Altoona nodded and waved her plump hands wildly. "Please take it away if it hasn't burned up. I don't want to have anything to do with it! I'm sure it's bad luck. I'm sure that's why lightning struck the attic. I don't know what I can say to you if it has been destroyed."

"Don't be foolish, Altoona," Captain Dan told her. "If the thing's burned to a crisp, then it's burned. But I'm not going to believe that it attracts bad luck."

He went over to a couple of firemen who were reeling hose into place on top of the fire engine. One of them came with him, and they went into the house together. A few moments later Susan saw the chief's white helmet at an empty window in the attic. He looked out and waved down.

"We've found it!" he called. "Can't tell what shape it's in till we get it outside."

Gene opened the car door and got out. Adam jumped out on the other side and came around as if to help him, but Gene pushed his hand away.

"I'm all right," he said, but there was no resentment in his voice. Moving a bit cautiously, he went up the front walk and waited there with Adam beside him.

Susan released herself gently from Miss Altoona's leaning arm. "I want to see," she said and ran over to join Gene and her brother.

"Did you hurt yourself when you tackled Adam?" she asked Gene.

He shrugged. "A little. But I had to stop your crazy brother."

Adam grinned at him. "You sure stopped me. I never saw a better tackle in a football game."

"You *were* foolish," Susan told her brother. "If Gene hadn't caught you in time, you might have been hurt up there."

"I know," Adam nodded, sobering a little. "I guess there are a few things about fires I need to learn. Gene says he'll teach me."

The firemen were coming downstairs now. The chief came out ahead of two of his men who were carrying a heavy, blackened chunk of wood between them. Susan gasped in dismay and moved up up in order to see. The darkened block of wood was the carved head that had once graced the prow of the *Flying Sarah*. Gene bent anxiously to examine it, and then looked up at his grandfather.

"I think it'll be all right. Mostly the burned part is at the back where it won't show much. The face is hardly touched."

The chief nodded. "Good enough. I guess it would take a lot bigger fire than this one to burn as solid a piece as this."

For the first time, Susan could view the figurehead clearly. How wonderful it must have looked in its place on the *Flying Sarah!* The wind-blown robes were gone now, and the bright paint that had once covered this brown and weathered wood. But the arch of the neck was still proud, the deep-set eyes still followed a distant horizon, and there was the stamp of courage and invincibility in the very lift of the chin.

At a signal from the chief, the two firemen lifted the head and carried it over to the chief's car, where Adam ran to open the trunk for them.

Susan watched for a moment longer. It was all over now, and the head had gone back to its proper owners. The day's excitement was done with, and Altoona Heath and her servants had hurried inside to have a look at the damage. Adam was still talking to Gene, as if they might really get to be friends. There was nothing for her to do around here. She might as well go down to the Old Oak and report what had happened to Aunt Edith.

As Susan started across the grass, she felt something hard and knobby under one foot, and she bent to pick up a strand of burned and blackened beads. They were all that remained of the necklace Captain Rufus had put about the neck of the figurehead. Being separate from the rest, they had burned more easily. The clasp had apparently broken, and when the head was dumped on the lawn, the strand had dropped off. Susan took the charred remains over to the Captain, who was still moving about the fire scene in his role of chief.

"These are the beads from the figurehead," she said. "Do you want them?"

The Captain glanced at the beads and shook his head. "We've a better set than that," he said, and returned his attention to the work still going on.

Susan thrust the blackened beads into a pocket of her jeans. In a way, they made a sort of souvenir, she thought, as she wiped her hands on a patch of wet grass. The excitement was over for now. But there was still tomorrow and the firemen's fair. It was all the more certain that Captain Dan would be re-elected as chief, after the successful handling of this fire.

She set off toward the shop, beginning to feel a little limp with reaction. A good many things had been cleared up today, but there were still questions she wanted to ask Gene. All the pieces had not yet fallen into place.

Aunt Edith was still in the shop. She had heard the siren and had known that the fire was nearby, so she was anxious to hear about it.

Susan did more than tell her the story of the fire. Whether Adam said so or not, she felt that the time had come to tell Aunt Edith about the carved head and the secret compartment. Her aunt was fascinated by her account, and she could hardly wait till they closed the shop and returned to the Teague house for dinner, so she could see the secret for herself.

Adam was there by that time, and Susan let him demonstrate. Aunt Edith watched, her eyes alight with interest.

"I wonder why it was hidden there?" she mused. "Why was it kept a secret all these years?"

"That's what I want to know," Susan said. "And that's what I mean to find out tomorrow."

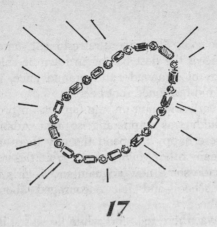

17

Firemen's Fair

On the Saturday of the fair there was no sultry threat in the air. It was a lovely, clear day—just warm enough, yet not uncomfortable.

Old clothes were the rule for this occasion, Aunt Edith said, since there would be games and stunts for anyone who wanted to take part in them. So Susan and Adam put on their jeans again before leaving.

Out behind the firehouse was a cleared field that had once been the playground of the school. Here booths had been set up and decorated, and both the permanent residents of Highland Crossing and most of the summer people had donated articles to be sold. There were refreshment stands too, with some of the best baking in town on sale, and large jugs of lemonade and orange juice, plus a barrel of old-fashioned root beer.

From early morning on, the fair was in progress, and enough was happening so that Adam and Susan were happy to spend the day there—as did a good many other young people from the vicinity. Susan made some new acquaintances—girls in her year at school—and felt encouraged about the months ahead.

Gene was there too, and while he was still a bit standoffish with the other boys, he no longer minded Adam. And once Susan overheard Adam bragging to some of the boys about what Gene had done yesterday to keep him from going into the burning house. Such words were good for Gene, and he seemed to straighten up a little under Adam's praise.

Perhaps everything would be better for Gene now, Susan thought. When school started, he wouldn't feel quite so left out with Adam around. Maybe he would even learn to face up to the fact that there were things he could do, and other things he couldn't.

The only sad thing in the picture was the Captain's need for money, which forced him to give up his home and live in that little cabin. Susan was afraid she would never be comfortable or carefree in the house that ought to belong to Captain Dan. But at least there was the anticipation of the Captain's pleasure in being elected once more as chief of the fire company at the end of the fair. Now nothing could spoil that.

In the afternoon, after everyone had sat around on campsite benches eating large picnic lunches purchased from the booths, the organized program began.

The volunteer firemen gave a demonstration of ladder-climbing and other feats, with the chief calling his orders through the big bull horn. Then there were games for both grown-ups and young people. Susan ran a couple of relay races without covering herself with much glory. One of the spectacles she most enjoyed was watching the boys' three-legged race. Adam picked Gene for a partner, and since Gene was quite used to getting around with one handicapped leg, he managed to drag Adam with him and win the race over the boys with two perfectly good legs.

Later, when the fair was almost over, Susan climbed up to sit beside Gene and Adam on a stone wall above the grounds. For once, Gene seemed relaxed and happy. This, she felt, was a good time to bring up certain questions that still tantalized her.

"Last night," she told him, "we showed Aunt Edith the secret compartment and told her all about the figurehead. But we've agreed not to tell anyone else. If you want it kept a secret, we'll help you. But why *do* you, Gene?"

"That's a good question," Adam said. "Why was the head hidden in that place anyway?"

Gene looked off toward the sloping curve of hill where Bear Mountain seemed to end the horizon, but he was clearly gazing into space without seeing anything before him.

"I guess there's no reason why you shouldn't know the story now," he mused. "It all began because of my great-great-great-grandmother, Sarah Teague. After Captain Rufus was killed by pirates on the *Flying Sarah,* she made herself a poor woman by paying off the debt of the jewels that the Captain had been commissioned to bring from India to his mandarin friend in Hong Kong. There was no insurance covering that transaction, and Sarah Teague felt it was an honorable debt that she had to pay off."

Gene paused to watch Miss Altoona down on the playground, where she had joined a game with some children who could move a great deal faster than she could. Evidently she had recovered from the shock of the fire, and Susan had never seen her look more cheerful than she did today. But it wasn't Miss Altoona who interested her now.

"Go on," she urged Gene.

"I was just trying to remember the details," he said. "After her husband's death, Sarah Teague decided to sell the *Flying Sarah* to help raise money, but first she gave orders that the figurehead was to be taken off. Her husband had carved it in what he considered her likeness, but I guess she always hated it. She felt she wasn't that ugly, and she just couldn't see how fine the carving really was. While

Rufus was captain of the ship, she couldn't prevent his using the figurehead as he had intended it, since he felt that it honored his wife. After he died, she didn't like the idea of another captain using it on a ship, so it was taken off and brought home.

"When they got it to Highland Crossing, it was too big to do anything with. Her son wouldn't let it be destroyed, and I guess even Sarah felt she couldn't have something her husband had worked over and prized discarded as trash. But she still wouldn't have it on exhibit some place where strangers could stare at it and think what an ugly-looking woman she had been. Grandfather says her son, who was his grandfather, had a sense of humor, and he also loved his mother a lot and admired her. So when he built his new house, he had a special secret compartment built in beside the fireplace in the living room. He and his brothers put it in themselves, so nobody outside the family would know about it. Grandfather says the figurehead was a sort of family joke in the beginning. It was there for the family to see, and not stuck away in an attic."

Adam shook his head doubtfully. "A pretty queer sort of joke!"

"Anyway," Gene said, "the figurehead was concealed in the secret compartment to make Sarah happy."

"But why," Susan asked, "did her descendants just go on doing as she wished?"

"She must have been a pretty strong-minded woman," Gene said. "And when she found she had a bad heart, she told her son that if he didn't keep the figurehead hidden in the family, she'd come back and haunt the house for all the generations ahead. I suppose she was just making a grim sort of joke. But her son humored her by putting it right into his will that it should be kept hidden. And he promised that his son would put it into his will too. Maybe not because he was afraid of being haunted, but to give his mother some peace—since she had a funny quirk about this. Anyway, all the Teagues who have inherited the house have kept the secret ever since."

Susan could almost see the stern-visaged Sarah setting down the beginnings of a legend that would continue through the years.

"Grandfather was the first one willing to break the chain," Gene said, and there was disapproval in his voice.

Susan stared at him. "What do you mean?"

"Grandfather thought the idea of keeping the secret was pretty silly by now. Especially if he had to sell the house. He said we could do one of three things: leave the figure where it was, and let someone discover it by accident, if it was discovered at all. Or we could tell the people who bought the house about the secret and let them do as they liked with it. Or, as a third choice, we could give the figurehead to a museum, since it has historical value now."

"Oh, you couldn't do that after the way Sarah felt!" Susan cried.

"No," Gene said, "I don't think we could. Grandfather still has a feeling about it that wouldn't let him do that. There was one more choice—the one I thought of, though I didn't tell him. I meant to take it out of the house before you moved in, and hide it somewhere until we had a place to keep it properly. But you moved in sooner than I expected. So I had to go back that very night and take it out. I used Grandfather's key and went in through the back door. But after the head bumped to the floor, I had to drag it out a window fast and get it away from the house."

So that was the story—and a strange one it was.

The three on the wall sat on in silence for a while. Events were coming to an end below. Visitors had begun to drift away. Women were packing up the things left at the booths, small children were growing tired and ready to cry, and the volunteer firemen, nearly all of whom had turned out for this occasion, were grouped in front of the firehouse, talking among themselves.

Susan saw Captain Dan coming toward them across the playground, looking graver than the occasion seemed to warrant. She would have expected him to be happy over the success of the fair, which must have raised a good deal of money for the coming year. Then she remembered that the election of the chief was still ahead, and perhaps he felt he mustn't look too cheerful and certain until this had been decided.

"I'd like to talk to you a minute, Gene," he said gravely.

The two walked off a little way together. Susan, watching, saw that Gene was listening solemnly to something his grandfather was saying. He didn't look at all pleased, and Susan wondered if all this had anything to do with the election.

When the firemen started up the steps into the meeting room, Gene left his grandfather and went with them. Captain Dan watched him go, and once, when Gene looked over his shoulder, the old man smiled at him, and Gene managed to smile back.

Then the Captain came to join Susan and Adam on the wall.

"It won't take long," he said. "Dropping those little balls through a slot goes pretty fast."

"Are you worried?" Adam asked him.

His smile was gentle and a little sad. "I'm not worried a bit," he said. "I think I know what's going to happen."

Susan felt better after that. She still felt she couldn't bear it if the Captain had to lose his house and the election, but surely that wouldn't happen.

Most of the children who had been playing with Miss Altoona had been taken off by their mothers, and now she, too, came over to the wall and sat down beside Susan. There was a dusty patch on the back of her skirt, where she had sat on the ground, and one of her stockings had a tear where she had fallen. She took off her sunglasses and straw hat, looking breathless and hot and quite happy.

"It's wonderful to make up your mind about something," she told them. "Adam, you put it right up to me the other day, and I'm going to do what you suggested."

"I can't remember suggesting anything," Adam said.

"I'm going to travel," Miss Altoona said. "I'm going to close up my house and take a trip around the world. I've always wanted to, and now I will."

Some of the people who had attended the fair and worked right through still lingered on the playground. They were mostly the wives and children of the volunteer firemen, waiting to see how the election came out. One woman smiled and called out to the Captain.

"My Bill's going to vote for you, Chief. And the rest of the boys will too. Everybody wants you to keep on with the good job you're doing."

The Captain nodded at her pleasantly, but he said nothing.

When the door to the firehouse opened and the men began to file down the steps, Susan knew at once that something had gone wrong. They looked solemn and troubled. Gene, who had the right to be among them as an honorary member of the company, came down very slowly, and there was an expression on his face as though he were close to tears. As he limped toward his grandfather, he made an effort to straighten his shoulders and control his unhappiness. When he reached the wall, he looked his grandfather straight in the eye.

"Well, boy?" Captain Dan asked gently.

"There was a blackball," Gene said. "Somebody voted against you. Most of the men are pretty upset about it. They're trying to figure out how to tell you."

The Captain rose from the wall and put a hand on his grandson's shoulder. "Thank you, Gene. I'll go talk to them."

He looked so brave and erect as he went toward them that Susan's heart twisted a little and tears came into her eyes.

"He wanted to keep on," Gene said grimly. "He wanted to keep on as chief more than anything. I hope I can be like he is some day."

"But who would vote against him?" Adam said indignantly.

Gene didn't speak for a long moment. Then he looked at Adam. "I did," he said.

Susan gasped, and Adam stared in astonishment.

Gene smiled ruefully at their expressions. "I guess you two can keep it to yourselves. I didn't do it because I wanted to. Grandfather told me I must."

"But—why?" Susan wailed.

"He knows that a younger man ought to be put in his place," Gene said. "But the men love him and they don't want to let him go. He tried to resign a while back, but they wouldn't have it. They told him he was better than any three younger men. He thinks that isn't true. It's getting hard for him to run things down here. The fire yesterday pointed that up more than ever. So he told me I had to vote against him. It was the only way. They'd have to respect a blackball. Now they'll have to find someone else to act as chief, and that'll take time. They'll get used to the idea and accept it."

Susan rubbed the back of her hand across her eyes. "I think it's awful! He's had to give up his house, and now he can't be fire chief, even though he loves the job. I don't want to live in your house, Gene! I want you to have it back!"

"You could move into mine," said an unexpected voice.

They had all forgotten Miss Altoona, and now the three of them stared at her in astonishment and dismay. She looked pink-cheeked with excitement.

"Oh, I won't tell," she said. "I have things to make up for, so you can count on me. But why can't you Prices and Edith Sperry just move into my house? I'll be away for a year or more, and as soon as the repairs are made you'll be perfectly comfortable. That would give you time to find another house you could buy. Then Gene and the Captain can move right back into their own house."

Gene smiled at her with unexpected warmth. "Thanks a lot, Miss Altoona. But I guess we need the money more than we need the house. I've been kind of an expense to everybody, and until I can find a way to make up for it, we'll have to stay in the cabin."

Susan knew she was going to cry now. The Captain was coming toward them across the playground and she couldn't bear to look at him; she couldn't bear any of this. She reached into her pocket for the handkerchief she hoped was there, and instead drew out the charred strand of beads that she had forgotten since she had found them yesterday. She couldn't mop her tears with wooden beads, and she ran them helplessly back and forth between her fingers, feeling the burned and brittle wood disintegrating at her touch.

"Hey!" Adam cried. "What've you got there?"

"It's just that burned necklace from the figurehead—" she began, and then looked at the strand in her hands.

In several places the beads were gone completely, and there were some hard, rather bright little lumps underneath. Adam took the strand from her hands and began to strip the beads away, dropping the burned bits of wood on the ground. The Captain had joined them, and they all stood in stunned silence watching Adam. With the wood stripped off, he rubbed what was left hard against his jeans and then dangled it before them. The shining bits on the chain he held danced and glittered like tiny rainbows in the air.

Captain Dan recovered himself first. "Let me see, boy," he said, and took the strand from Adam to turn it about in his fingers. "So that's what happened! Captain Rufus hid them after all," he said softly. "I always wondered why he didn't when he knew the danger of pirates in those seas. Especially when the jewels weren't insured."

"Wh-what are they?" Susan whispered.

"I think we have a diamond and emerald necklace here," the captain said, and held out the strand for them to see.

Each gem had been set in a tiny individual setting of what was probably gold, and each setting had been secured to what must be a gold chain.

Susan bent to pick up a charred bead from the

ground and held it out to the Captain. The answer was clear. Captain Rufus had evidently taken the time to hollow out each bead so that it could be strung right over the diamond necklace. Then he had fastened the wooden beads around the neck of the figurehead where no one would ever question them. Undoubtedly he had expected to remove them himself when the ship docked safely in Hong Kong.

Captain Dan whistled softly as he examined the bead Susan had handed him. "He wrote the clue into his log too," he said to Gene. "But nobody ever saw the sense of it. Remember—?"

Gene nodded. "He said the new beads he had carved were too fine to be left on the neck of the figurehead. But nobody understood, and after he was killed, nobody wanted to take them off."

"A fortune sailing the seas around the neck of a wooden figurehead," Captain Dan mused.

"But now they belong to us, don't they?" Gene asked, sounding a little breathless.

The Captain nodded. "Bought and paid for by our ancestors a good many years ago."

It was Miss Altoona who broke the spell that lay upon them. She began to polish her sunglasses in nervous excitement, although the sun was disappearing behind the hills.

"As I was saying, you Prices might just as well move out of the Teague house and into mine as soon as the repairs are finished," she said triumphantly. "I don't know anybody who would take better care of my treasures than Edith Sperry."

Gene and the Captain looked at each other, and the Captain nodded.

"Maybe things will work out after all, boy. But even when we know what this is worth, there'll be no wild spending. There's college ahead for you, and a start in what you decide to do with your life."

"Mother can come up here to live with us now," Gene added with a break in his voice, and Susan knew how much he had missed her.

But now she felt that Gene and his grandfather should be left alone to savor all this for themselves and to make plans for the future. She poked Adam, who still looked a bit stunned.

"Come along," she said. "Let's go tell Aunt Edith."

He understood quickly, and they waved to the others and started off toward the Old Oak. But Gene's voice stopped them before they had taken more than a few steps.

"Wait a minute!" he called, and he came after them, walking better than Susan had ever seen him manage. When they stopped and he came up to them, he looked a little embarrassed, but very happy. "I—I just wanted to say thanks to you both," he told them. "If it hadn't been for you, Susan, we might never have found the necklace. When you saw that face in the pool you started more than you knew. And Adam—" he hesitated awkwardly, "next week maybe we could go fishing in a good place I know."

Adam grinned his pleasure, and Susan knew that Gene was thanking him for a lot more than his part in the discovery of the jewels, for more than he could put into words.

Gene stood at the edge of the road and looked after them as they crossed. Susan could hardly wait to get to the Old Oak and tell Aunt Edith about what had happened.

No one would be hurt now. Dad could come up here as soon as the doctors would let him—and Mom and the boys as well. She felt as though she might bubble over with sheer happiness at the prospect.

"You know what?" Adam said as they reached the shop. "This town isn't half bad, at that."

Susan smiled, knowing that he felt just what she was feeling, but as a boy he said it differently. This town—the hills, the river, the woods, the ponds and, most of all, the people—belonged to her now, and to Adam. And she and Adam belonged to them. What a wonderful way to end a summer!

Biography of Phyllis A. Whitney

PHYLLIS WHITNEY lives on a hilltop in Staten Island out in the harbor of New York. To reach Manhattan she must cross the harbor by ferryboat—a half-hour ride each way. Thus the mouth of the Hudson River, opening as it does not far from the place where the ferry docks, is a familiar sight to her.

Especially interesting to her are the little towns along the river—many of them older than America's freedom, and each with a life and history of its own. The section of the Hudson where the river narrows and curves sharply between hills that rise on either bank has long been known in story and legend for its beauty—the Hudson Highlands. It was to this part of the river that Miss Whitney went when she decided to write about a small Hudson River town.

Fort Montgomery was the real town she visited to gather her background material, though she used bits of other towns as well to make up her imaginary "Highland Crossing." In Fort Montgomery she found the volunteer library she describes in the story, and she also found a volunteer fire company, occupying an old schoolhouse. The activities of this fire company were wonderfully interesting, and very soon the plot of *Mystery of the Haunted Pool* began to grow in her mind.